DEAD RITE

A mystery novel by

JIM GILMORE

contemporary press

This is a work of fiction. All of the characters and events portrayed in this book are either products of the author's twisted imagination or are used ficticiously.

Dead Rite

Cover Design by Chris Reese

A Contemporary Press Book
Published by Contemporary Press
Brooklyn, New York

Distributed by Publishers Group West
www.pgw.com

www.contemporarypress.com

ISBN 0-9744614-7-4

First edition: February 2005

Printed in the United States of America

For Sally

DEAD RITE

A mystery novel by

JIM GILMORE

If once a man indulges himself in murder,
very soon he comes to think very little of robbing;
and from robbing he next comes to drinking
and Sabbath-breaking,
and from that to incivility and procrastination

—Thomas De Quincey

1

Samuel Shelton leaned on the balcony railing of his luxury Beverly Hills high-rise apartment watching the blood-red sun begin its slow descent through the smog to the Pacific. Although he didn't know it, this was to be his last California sunset. He took a sip from the lowball glass of 100-proof Absolut on the rocks, and for a long moment, he stood gazing at the darkening January sky.

A mogul in a town of moguls, Shelton had just turned fifty-six, yet he had somehow succeeded in remaining true to his generation. He still didn't trust anyone over thirty, and he dressed casually in latter-day hippie: Reeboks, pleated jeans, and a lightweight denim shirt. The top three buttons of the shirt were purposely left undone to expose the curly salt-and-pepper hair of his chest and the gold chains that dangled from his neck. It was a style he had consciously made his uniform.

Shelton downed the last of the vodka, chewed the ice, and with a sigh of resignation turned to enter his apartment. He still had a lot of packing to do. He headed for the master bedroom and placed the empty glass on the dresser next to a picture of him embracing Sharon Grant, star of 1994's biggest hit, the *Sharon Grant Show*. Against his better judgment, he picked up the silver frame and allowed himself a wistful smile, remembering the good times. He wiped a smudge off the glass with his thumb, turned the picture face down on the dresser with a grunt, and strode into his walk-in closet. The red digital numerals on his nightstand glowed 5:43 p.m.

"Shit," he muttered. His flight to Honolulu left LAX at 8:30. Shelton hated that he had wasted so much time waiting for her to call. She was a good lay—one of the best he'd ever had—but if she didn't want to fly to the other side of the world with him, screw her. Hadn't he killed for her? What the hell was she trying to prove? She'd tire of trying to live the straight life, and by the time he returned from Tokyo, she'd be back in his apartment. In the meantime, there was a whole new country of good lays waiting for him across the Pacific.

It took Shelton less than five minutes to cram into a travel-worn bag all the essentials he needed for his two weeks in Hawaii and Japan. All he needed to survive anywhere in the world was a pocket full of plastic and a thirty-day supply of FiberCon, Flomax, Ambien, and Viagra in his toilet kit to help him shit, pee, sleep, and have a ball.

Shelton hefted his bag from the bed. If he was going to make his flight, he couldn't keep the moron down in the garage waiting any longer. The phone rang before he reached the bedroom door.

"Yes!" Shelton hissed, throwing his fist in the air. He knew she'd call. The caller ID on his phone showed an anonymous call. Where the fuck was she calling from? He let it ring two more times before hitting the talk button. It never paid to appear too anxious, especially when dealing with talent.

"Hi, beautiful!" he answered cheerily.

"Samuel Shelton?" a deep, male voice asked.

"Who is this?"

"My name's Hicks. Deputy Hicks. I'm with the San Bernardino County Sheriff's Department—"

"How'd you get through on this line? All my calls are screened."

"Sorry, sir, but we need your help."

"Look. If you're selling tickets to a Sheriff's ball or something, put them in the mail and bill me. I gotta catch a flight to Honolulu."

"I'm investigating a homicide, sir. Don't hang up."

Shelton's face flushed, and he cleared his throat. "Homicide? Murder?"

"A double murder."

"Ah, how can I help?"

"Just answer a few questions."

"All right. But make it quick."

"Do you own a cabin on Big Bear Lake?"

"Yeah, my company does. So?"

"Do you know a Gordon Duffy?"

"Gordon? Yeah, he's my partner."

"Then I'm afraid I've got some very bad news for you."

"Bad news?"

"There's no easy way to say this, sir ..."

"Say what?"

"Your partner's dead."

Shelton sank onto the bed. "Dead? You gotta be kidding. What is this, some kind of sick joke?"

"I assure you, Mr. Shelton, it's no joke." The man had a curious squeak to his voice. "A male victim tentatively identified as Gordon Duffy and a woman we think was his wife were found dead in your company cabin at Big Bear Lake this afternoon."

"Oh, God. I can't believe it ..."

"Believe me, sir. We've got two bodies up there. Both victims were shot in the head."

"In the head? Oh shit. That's terrible! But murder? It couldn't be murder—"

"It has to be," the officer chuckled. "There was no weapon in the bedroom. But we did find a .30-30 deer rifle on the living room floor. We believe it's the weapon that killed them."

"You sure? I mean, is it really Gordon and Jen?"

"The bodies haven't been positively identified yet. That's why I called. I'd sure appreciate it if you could drive up here and make the ID."

"Yeah ... I'll, uh, drive right up." Shelton clenched his teeth and closed his eyes. He needed another Absolut, preferably a double, but he'd had a stiff one already, and now he had to drive all the way to San Bernardino to meet a cop. He took a deep breath, trying to quell the anger, but it spilled out anyway.

"Goddamn it! Why did this have to happen? I'm supposed to be on an 8:30 flight to Hawaii!"

"Sorry, sir. I know it's an inconvenience. Murder always is. But we really do need your help. You can meet me here at the Sheriff's Department."

Shelton's hand was shaking so badly he had trouble removing the gold pen from its holder on the note pad by the phone. He scrawled the directions as best he could.

"Traffic won't be too bad on a Saturday evening. Shouldn't take you more than an hour and a half or so," the officer assured him.

Glancing at his Rolex, Shelton answered, "It's a little before 6:00. I should be there about 7:30 or 8:00."

"Better bring along a warm jacket. Nights can be cold up at Big Bear this time of year."

"Any time of year," Shelton agreed.

"Just one more thing, sir—"

"Yeah?"

"Until we have a positive ID, I'd appreciate it if you didn't tell anyone about this. There's always the possibility it's not your partner or his wife. We do make mistakes."

"I hope to shit you have."

Shelton hung up and immediately tried to call his secretary at home to have her cancel his reservations, but after two rings, he changed his mind. She was sure to ask why he'd changed his plans, and he couldn't tell her. He couldn't tell anyone.

4

2

Because it was a Saturday, the Sheriff's Department visitor lot in San Bernardino was almost deserted when Sam Shelton's green Jaguar XK8 arrived forty-five minutes late. A dark blue SUV was parked just beyond the entrance. As the Jaguar passed it, a tall man in a black leather jacket climbed out, headed to the Jaguar on foot, and pushed a number into a cell phone. When a male voice answered, he grinned, hung up, and walked up to the Jaguar as it pulled into a space. Before Shelton could turn off the ignition, the man tapped on the driver's side window with the butt-end of a flashlight. As the electric window rolled down, he shined the light into Shelton's eyes. Shelton threw his hands up, squinted, and saw *DEPUTY* written in white letters across the front of the blue base-ball cap.

"Hicks?"

"Mr. Shelton? Lock your vehicle and give me the keys, sir. We'll drive up to Big Bear in my truck."

Shelton got out and locked his car as he was told. He never questioned the motives of a cop unless he was arguing a ticket, so he obediently handed over his keys and followed the deputy to his SUV.

Climbing in, Shelton shook his head, saying, "Lincoln Navigator? You running guns on the side? Never knew you cops had it so good."

"Luck of the draw," the deputy said. "It's the only one available from the department pool tonight." He took off his cap, placing it on the console between them. By the light of the overhead lamp, Shelton saw that his driver was lean and fit, the perfect cliché of an officer of the law.

"Got to check in with the office. You have a cell phone?"

———

Ten minutes later, the Navigator was snaking its way up City Creek Road, north of Highland. The two men had fallen silent, but the deputy finally broke the ice. "Too bad you had to give up your Hawaii trip."

Shelton sighed. "Yeah. Well, actually, I was going to Tokyo. It's a fourteen-hour flight, and I get claustrophobia if I'm cooped up too long. So, I was spending a couple of days in Honolulu to break up the trip."

"Business or pleasure?"

"Business. I was going to receive an award for my company at the Tokyo Fair Game. That's Japlish for Game Fair."

"Stupid gooks," the deputy put in, surprising Shelton.

"Yeah, they're real arrogant shits to do business with, but the women are great pieces of ass."

"What business you in again?"

Shelton had a stock answer ready. "Games are my game. I'm the President of GameCo. We design and market video games."

"Like Nintendo?"

"Yeah. *Quicksand* ... *Craven Images* ... *Dead Rite* ... they're all ours."

"You dream up the games?"

Shelton shook his head. "No, I'm not nuts enough to be a designer. Duffy and his wife, Jen, head the design team. Shit, I still can't believe they're gone. They were the goddamn best. Impossible to replace."

"I'm sorry for your loss."

"Thanks for the standard-issue sympathy." Shelton took out a box of Marlboro's. "Mind if I smoke?"

"Yes."

Shelton shrugged and stuffed the box of Marlboros back in his shirt pocket. "Funny," Shelton said, almost to himself, looking out his window.

The deputy gave him a sidelong glance. "Funny?"

"That Jen was with Gordon, I mean."

"How's that?"

"The Big Bear cabin was mostly Gordon's retreat; a place where he could get away from it all. Work out the bugs of a game. Jen was a city girl, a Brit from London, originally. She hated the isolation of the place. Hardly ever went up there with him."

They passed a 6,000-feet-above-sea-level sign, and a steady drizzle began to fall as they entered a bank of scud. The deputy turned on the thumping windshield wipers.

The deputy said, "We assumed the woman we found in bed with Duffy was his wife. Maybe she wasn't. Your partner fool around?"

"No way. If anyone was—" Shelton stopped and threw his arms to protect his face. "Oh, shit!" he yelled, as the glare of two headlights suddenly came out of the mist, heading right at them.

———

Wrenching the wheel to the right, the deputy hit the brakes. The SUV fish-tailed left, almost rolled over, and careened to the right, tires yowling before it crunched to a stop on the narrow gravel shoulder just short of the ditch.

Unbuckling his seat belt, the deputy grunted, "You all right?"

"Guess so," was all Shelton could manage.

The deputy opened his door, peering back across the road at

the other vehicle. It had skidded to a stop on the opposite shoulder, about fifty yards down the road.

"Goddamn idiot!" he spat, climbing out of the SUV.

"Asshole must be drunk," Shelton agreed, unbuckling his seat belt. He opened his door.

"Stay in the vehicle," the deputy ordered, raising his voice. "I'll handle it."

Shelton watched him cross the road to the vehicle that had sideswiped them: a beat up old Jeep Cherokee. He knew it was wrong, but the asshole in the Jeep nearly took them out—so, he ignored the deputy's orders and climbed out the door. The night air was cold. Zipping up his bomber jacket, he circled to the back of the Navigator to check the driver's side. The collision sounded worse than it was; there was only a small foot-long scrape on the back panel. He wondered if the Cherokee had gotten off so easy and decided to check it out. Halfway across the road, his foot kicked something metallic. He stooped to pick it up. It was a broken car door handle. Clutching the handle, he strode up behind the deputy who was standing next to the Jeep, arguing with its driver.

"Look, you say it's my fault. I say it's yours," the driver fumed, slurring his words. "If you got a cell phone, call the goddamn Sheriff—"

"Just your luck, pal," Shelton interrupted. "He's a deputy."

The deputy turned on him. "Mr. Shelton! I told you to stay in the vehicle."

"Fuck," the other driver groaned. "You're a deputy?"

"You've got it," Shelton told him.

"You deaf?" the deputy asked Shelton, growing angrier.

"Just curious."

A huge semi roared up out of the mist, its lights almost blinding Shelton and the deputy. The truck's air horn blasted them as it thundered past before disappearing into the mist again.

"Curiosity kills!" the deputy shouted at Shelton. "We could all be run down in this fog. Now, get back to my vehicle. You'll be safer there."

Shelton recoiled at being told what to do, but the guy was a cop, so he sighed, turned, and retreated across the road, absently pocketing the door handle. He sat in the SUV almost five minutes before he heard the Jeep drive off into the mist. Seconds later, the deputy opened the driver's side door and slid in, slipping a piece of note paper under the driver's side visor.

"Give the asshole a ticket?" Shelton asked.

"Let him off with a warning." The deputy buckled up and started the engine.

Shelton couldn't believe it. "You let a drunk like that off with just a warning?"

"He's not that drunk. I got his name and address. I'll talk to him tomorrow."

"Tomorrow? Shit, he could kill somebody tonight."

"I'm a homicide detective, not a traffic cop," the deputy snapped, pulling back onto the highway.

———

They topped the scud as they passed the 7,000-foot marker, and the deputy switched off the windshield wipers. The air was so crisp and clear the stars barely twinkled. Shelton didn't notice. It suddenly hit him what he was about to do, and his mind started wandering in an inner gloom. The idea of having to identify the Duffys' bodies was depressing him more and more the closer they got to Big Bear. He wondered how he'd react when he saw them. Would their faces be blown away? The thought made him shiver. "How much further to the hospital?" he finally asked.

"Not going to the hospital."

"Isn't that where the bodies are?"

"They have to remain at the scene until the crime lab and the coroner's people are finished with them."

"Goddamn. The bodies have been at the cabin since this afternoon?"

"Yes, and they'll be there until they're released to the medical examiner."

Shelton turned and stared out his side window again. For the first time, he saw the full moon rising above the pines. The sight didn't improve his mood. He hadn't been up to the cabin since his wife's death four years ago, and now death was drawing him there again. He rubbed his eyes and checked his Rolex. It was 10:42 when they rounded a bend in the road, and the headlights picked up a mailbox with "Last Resort" spelled out in silver Scotchlite.

"Hey, you missed the turn. That was our mailbox," he told the deputy.

The deputy nodded, slowing the SUV. "Your drive's blocked with coroner and Sheriff's Department vehicles. There's a service road just ahead."

"Shows you how often I come up here. Never knew we had a service road."

The deputy shifted into four-wheel drive and turned into a rutted dirt side road that was almost overgrown with weeds. They bounced along through the pines for a few hundred yards before the deputy braked to a stop at the top of a ravine that led down to the lake. He turned out the lights. Through the bug-splattered windshield, Shelton could see the water of the lake sparkling in the bright moonlight below them. The deputy clicked on the overhead light, reached into the center console, and pulled out a .38 revolver with a silencer already screwed into the barrel. He pointed the gun at Shelton's head. "Get the fuck out!"

Shelton's eyes bulged at the gun just inches from his face, believing that a cop had no right to point his weapon at a law-abiding citizen. "You nuts?"

"Do as you're told, and you won't get hurt."

Shelton's head was spinning. "Do what?"

"Get out."

It was impossible for Shelton to move. Nothing worked. His arms and legs clenched against the seat and they began to shake, along with his stomach. It was all he could do to gasp, "You're crazy!"

"I said, get out!"

"Please!"

A foul odor filled the SUV as Shelton emptied his bowels into the seat of his pants.

"Jesus Christ!" The deputy slapped him across the side of his face with the gun, got out, and walked to the passenger-side door.

Shelton had bit his tongue, and he began to bleed from the mouth.

"Don't bleed on the fucking seats, too!" the deputy yelled, grabbing the collar of Shelton's bomber jacket and pulling him out the door.

Shelton fell to the ground, rolled up into the fetal position, and whimpered, "Please! Please!" as he took a few sharp kicks in the ribs.

"Get the fuck up!" the deputy ordered. When Shelton still didn't move, he was yanked to his feet and slammed against the side of the SUV.

Tears and blood streaked Shelton's face. "You're going to kill me!"

"Not if you shut up and do what I say." He spun Shelton around, jabbed the gun in his ribs, and ordered, "Move to the back of the vehicle!"

"Why are you doing this?" Shelton sniveled.

The deputy swung open the rear cargo door. "There's a shovel inside. Take it out."

Shelton reached inside the cargo bay, fumbling for the shovel. When his trembling hands found the hilt, he gripped it firmly, and the pressure helped to steady him. Slowly, he slid the shovel from the bay. His fear was turning to anger. He spun around, raising the shovel to swing it.

"Don't," the deputy warned.

Shelton dropped the shovel. Suddenly, his stomach trembled,

but this time, he doubled over and vomited, crying, "Oh, God! Please help me!"

"Pick up the shovel. You've got some digging to do."

"But I'm fucking sick!"

"You'll be a lot sicker if you don't do as you're told."

Shelton blew the vomit out of his nose and picked up the shovel. With a gun in his ribs, he was marched down the ravine toward the lake. The short walk gave him the time to wonder what was really happening to him. It felt like a crazy dream, but then again, maybe it was God repaying him for what he did to his ex-wife. And as soon as religion entered the equation, he thought *Please, dear God, wake me up. I can't take any more.*

"Far enough," the man finally said, stopping Shelton at a small hummock in the pines. "Dig."

Shelton put his foot on the spade and pushed it into the damp, cold earth.

"Your name really Hicks?"

The man didn't answer.

"You're not a deputy, are you?"

Still no answer.

"Did someone hire you to kill me?"

The man merely laughed; the same squeal Shelton heard on the phone.

"Stop playing games with me."

Finally the man spoke, "I thought games were your game."

"Did you kill Gordon and Jen?"

"Who said they were dead?"

"You did."

"You believe everything you hear? Now save your breath and dig. I'd like to get a little sleep before the night is over."

———

Midnight came and went while Shelton continued to dig the hole exactly as instructed. The ground was soft and sandy, yet it was tough, physical work, and it had been years since Shelton had worked with his hands. The skin of his soft palms quickly blistered; the blisters broke, and the skin peeled away, but he went on digging, afraid of what would happen if he stopped. The hole was now about three feet deep, almost as wide, and a little more than five feet long. Shelton wondered how much deeper, wider, and longer he would be ordered to dig it. He hated taking orders almost as much as he hated real work.

Shelton always considered himself a master when it came to playing mind games. He knew he was digging his own grave, but his thoughts raced as he shoveled to figure out why. Was it because of Mary? He'd planned his wife's death, but no one could be sure of that. And yes, he could be ruthless in business, but that's the only way to play the game. Now, his problem was worse: there were no rules with this guy. Just like a video game, Shelton realized he had to think ahead. Use his brain. Try alternatives. Outsmart the silicon. Stay calm. Stall for time. He stopped digging and looked up at the deputy who was standing on the mound of dirt he had shoveled from the hole.

"Can I take a break?" Shelton wheezed.

"Keep digging."

"My hands are raw."

"You're almost finished. It's deep enough. Just make it a little longer."

Shelton dug. "You owe me an explanation."

"I don't owe you a thing. Dig."

Shelton began digging his way toward the deputy. Maybe he could catch him off guard, throw a shovel of dirt in his face and blind him. It was a rookie move, but he had to do something.

"I'm taking a cigarette break."

The deputy laughed. "Smoking's bad for your health."

Shelton took a Marlboro box from his shirt pocket.

"Go ahead. Kill yourself."

Being positive seemed to be working. Shelton lit up, blowing out a stream of smoke. He held the box out to the man. "Want one?"

"Gave it up."

Shelton knew he had to keep the deputy talking about himself. "Wish I could. He took another, deeper drag. "I quit about twenty times; swore it off every night, right after I snuffed out the last butt of the day. The next morning, I'd light up again, even before I got out of bed."

"That's how it was with me."

"So, how'd you stop?"

"Hypnosis."

"You're kidding?" Shelton was still leaning casually on the shovel, but as he took another deep drag, he pushed the head of the spade a little deeper into the loose dirt with his foot. "Does that really work?"

"Did for me."

"Maybe I should see a hypnotist." Shelton was waiting for just the right moment to throw the dirt.

"If you do, don't see a quack."

Shelton considered that a positive statement. "Oh?"

"I went to a shrink. The best there is. He told me it'd take five visits before I stopped. I thought he was full of shit. All we seemed to do was talk. Sports, the weather—crap like that. The only thing we didn't discuss was cigarettes and smoking; and I was paying a hundred bucks a crack. The third visit, I complained, and he smiled and started telling me stuff about myself I'd never told him. At least not consciously. The fifth visit, he taught me to hypnotize myself."

"You're shitting me." Shelton leaned forward on the shovel, then back, wiggling the head of the spade to loosen the dirt even more.

"Whenever I'm going into a tense situation, I relax and reinforce my negative feelings about smoking. Damned if it doesn't work. I never smoked again after that fifth visit. I still hypnotize myself whenever I need it."

"Maybe I should see him. Where's his office? L.A.?"

"No."

Shelton took one last drag on his cigarette and dropped it into the dirt, grinding it out with his foot. A light breeze had the pines murmuring. The swaying boughs filtered the bright moonlight streaming through them, creating shadows that danced about the ravine like ghosts in a graveyard. Shelton told himself it was now or never. He tightened his grip on the shovel's hilt.

"Don't even think about it," the deputy said, reading his mind.

The words were like a slap in the face for Shelton, snapping him back to reality.

"What's the shrink's name?" he said, trying to start up the small talk again.

"You won't need him." The man raised the revolver. He steadied it with both hands and cocked the hammer with his thumb. "I can guarantee you'll never smoke again."

Shelton had just enough time to blink.

There was soft pop, and a bright orange tongue of fire erupted from the .38's silencer. Samuel Shelton's universe exploded like a star being swallowed up by a black hole.

The killer shined his flashlight on the body in the grave and grinned at his handiwork. A neat hole had been drilled in Shelton's forehead just above the left eye where the slug entered his brain, turning its gray matter into pinkish mush and oozing out the massive exit wound at the back of his head. The killer placed the flashlight next to the grave, tucked the revolver into his belt, picked up the spade, and began to cover Samuel Shelton's still-twitching body with dirt.

3

It was almost 2:00 a.m. by the time the killer returned to the SUV at the top of the ravine. He tossed the spade in back and climbed in behind the wheel. He had to make another stop before he called it a night. Flipping down the driver's side visor, he opened the slip of paper and read the name and address of the man who side-swiped them in the Jeep Cherokee. Harry Perz. Route 330, a few miles below Running Springs. He stuffed the paper in his shirt pocket, turned the SUV around, and by the light of the full moon, he drove slowly up the service road to the empty highway.

Twenty minutes later, he spotted Harry Perz's mailbox just below the peak of Harrison Mountain. Next to it was a *Firewood for Sale* sign. A gravel drive snaked back into a grove of tall ponderosa. He turned off the headlights and backed up the drive just far enough to hide the SUV from the highway.

He pulled on a pair of latex surgical gloves, inhaled deeply a few times, and switched on his flashlight. His ice-blue eyes reflect-ed in the rearview mirror as he began counting backwards from one hundred. By the time he reached ninety-two, he was ready. He turned off the flashlight, climbed out of the SUV, and started up the drive, holding the Smith & Wesson close to his side.

Cautiously, he moved deeper into the woods, staying off the gravel to keep his footfalls from being heard over the moaning of the wind in the pines. The drive led to a small clearing, ringed by stacks of split firewood. Perz's beat up Cherokee was parked next to an aging house trailer mounted on pillars of log blocks. Moving to the shadows beside the Cherokee, he surveyed the scene in the moonlight.

Perz was obviously sleeping. There were no lights in the trailer windows; no sign of any activity inside. He circled, taking care to avoid the litter scattered about the yard. The windows were small—too small for anyone to climb in or out—and the door was the only exit. He scanned the clearing and noticed a small tool shed and an outhouse about fifty feet beyond the trailer. Perz obviously made his living selling firewood. The shed would contain the tools of his trade: axes, chainsaws, gasoline....

The moon ducked behind a cloud. He headed for the shed, senses keenly alert, but he never saw the sleeping German shepherd tethered to a long chain in the shadows by the shed door. Because the dog was upwind, it didn't sense him until he stumbled on its metal food dish. The sound startled them both. Instinctively, the man thrust the .38 toward the sound of the dog's snarl. The dog leaped at it, clamping its jaws on the barrel. The man jerked back his hand, reflexively squeezing the trigger. The silencer and the dog's muzzle muffled the sound of the shot; and the slug ripped down the shepherd's throat, exploding its heart.

"Fuck!" the killer gasped, his own heart pounding in his ears. The shepherd lay crumpled at his feet. "Stupid fucking dog!" he muttered. He hated all animals, and his trembling hands snapped on his flashlight to find just a trickle of blood dripping from the dog's shattered mouth. He switched off the light, looked over his shoulder at the trailer, and waited for any sign that the shot had awakened Perz. None came.

The adrenalin made him dizzy. His mind raced. One of the .38's slugs was deep in the dog's body, so he had to get rid of it. There was no time to bury it, so he tucked the .38 into his belt and unbuckled the bloody collar. He dragged the shepherd into the outhouse. It was a three-holer, reeking of urine and shit. He held his breath, hoisted the dog by its hindquarters, and stuffed it down the middle hole.

The killer found everything he needed in the tool shed: a five-gallon can of gasoline with a flexible spout, a box of wooden matches, a framing hammer and some twenty-penny nails, oily rags, empty beer bottles, car wash detergent, and a funnel. He stuffed what he needed into an old gunnysack and carried it all to the far side of the Cherokee. By the light of the moon, he filled the beer bottles with gasoline and detergent, shook them up, and stuffed rags down their necks. He poured the rest of the gasoline under the Cherokee and the trailer, soaking the wood blocks that supported it. Moving quickly to the trailer's door, he began nailing it shut. There was a stirring inside, but he kept pounding. A light blinked. Perz's anxious face appeared in the door's round window.

"Who the fuck's out there?" he yelled. "I got a gun in here!"

"Fireman," the man screeched, pounding in one last spike.

"There's no fire here," Perz shouted.

"Wrong!"

The man ran to the beer bottles, lit the rags, and threw two bottles under the trailer. There was a loud, sucking sound and a blast of heat just as he threw the third bottle at the Cherokee and ran. The Jeep exploded in an orange fireball, and the terrified screams of Perz and some woman faded away as he sprinted down the gravel drive. He hadn't counted on anyone being in the trailer with Perz, but he decided that this was their bad luck, not his. He leaped into the SUV, and it roared out of the woods onto Route 330, heading down the mountain toward San Bernardino.

4

Weather-wise, it had been a fitful week at Big Bear. El Niño was playing tricks on Southern California. After an early morning shower, Sunday turned clear, crisp and cold. Monday and Tuesday there were snow showers. Wednesday and Thursday it poured. Friday was partly cloudy and warm for January, the high reaching almost seventy degrees. Saturday started out as another promising day, the temperature climbing with the sun. By 10:00 a.m., it had passed sixty degrees, and out on the lake, Gordon Duffy shed his windbreaker and unbuttoned his fisherman's vest as he sat in his red canoe just beyond the drop-off a few hundred feet down the shore from his cabin. There was a self-satisfied smile on his craggy face.

Duffy was smiling, but it wasn't because the fish were biting. They weren't. It was the sight of the woman walking the beach with a black Labrador retriever that brought the smile to his lips. Like most men, Duffy was a voyeur and on this day, Jennifer moved among the rocks less than fifty feet from where he sat in his canoe. She wore tight-knit leggings and a white Irish fisherman's sweater that brought out the best of what lay beneath: round, firm breasts; lean, long legs, and a saucy ass. "Pretty cheeky broad," he marveled to himself. He was lucky to have such an enticing wife.

"Any luck?" she called out to him.

"Not a nibble. Where're you off to?"

"Letting Rufus drag me through the woods."

"Why don't you let him off the leash?"

"And have him roll on some dead animal? No way. Bugger smells bad enough in his natural state. And put your hat on, luv. You know how your bald spot burns."

"*Thin* spot," he corrected her, suddenly testy from the reminder of the difference in their ages. Still, Duffy let his eyes follow Jen's ass as the lab led her along the beach.

He cast his lure onto a lily pad near the shore and let the Hula Popper sit there for a few seconds to tantalize the lunker he hoped was waiting just beyond the drop-off below. Then he whipped it off the pad and began reeling in the line, twitching the tip of his rod every second or two to make the popper pop. He was about to cast again when he saw Jen turn away from the lake, heading for a ravine that wound uphill through the rocks and pines.

"Jen!" he shouted.

She turned back to him. "What, luv?"

"Don't go up there. It'll be swarming with mosquitoes after all the rain."

She waved off his warning. "I'm saturated with repellant."

"When you get your smart ass bitten off, don't say I didn't warn you."

After she and the dog disappeared into the woods, Duffy decided to change his luck by changing lures. He put the rod down and opened his tackle box, looking for the plastic night crawler. It was turning out to be a great weekend. Jen seemed happy to be at the cabin with him again, and that made him happy.

———

He tied on the plastic worm and cast it into deeper water, letting it sink for a few seconds before he began to slowly reel it in. A yank on the line bent the tip of his rod down until it almost touched the water, and the spinning reel began to sing. A lunker broke water less than ten feet from the canoe; it was a monster bass, the mother of all largemouths. Then he heard it: a scream. The mother of all screams. Duffy looked toward the ravine where Jen and Rufus had disappeared minutes before. The scream came again, sounding even more terrified. Rufus was barking wildly; Duffy dropped the rod and picked up his paddle.

Jen ran from the ravine as he beached the canoe. "Oh, God, Gordon!" she cried hysterically. "Up ... up in the woods ... it's awful ... horrible!"

He ran up the beach and put his arms around her. Her body was shaking uncontrollably.

"Stop Rufus!" she sobbed. "Stop him!"

"What is it? A skunk?"

"No, no! A hand!"

"A what?"

"A *hand*!" Don't you understand? Oh, God!" she groaned, pulling away from him. "I'm going to throw up!" She bent over and was sick.

He held her by the waist until she stopped retching. "What the hell is Rufus barking at?"

She wiped her mouth with the back of her hand. "I told you, dammit! A *hand*! Stop him. He's trying to dig up the rest of it."

"Of what?"

"A *body*!" She retched again and gagged, "Rufus found a hand sticking up from a mound of dirt. Now he's trying to dig up the rest of it. Oh, God! What if he eats it?"

"Jesus Christ! Okay. Stay here." Duffy left her on the beach and ran up the ravine toward the sound of the barking. He found Rufus near the top of the ravine furiously digging into a mound of dirt.

"Damn it, Rufus!" he shouted. "Get the hell away from there!" He grabbed the leash, yanked the Lab back from the mound, and saw a bloated hand and the lower part of an arm unearthed. The stench brought the taste of bile to his mouth. He dragged Rufus away from the grave and down the ravine to the beach where Jen was waiting, still horrified.

"It is a body, isn't it?" she sobbed.

He took her by the arm and steered her down the beach toward the cabin. "I'll call the police."

Jen moaned, doubled over, and spilled the rest of her lunch into the sand.

5

Gordon Duffy's 911 call was logged in by the Big Bear Sheriff's station dispatcher, a small station with only twelve full-time deputies to serve more than 6,000 residents and the throngs of vacationers who visit the mountain resort area every year. Twenty minutes later, two public safety officers from the Big Bear Sheriff's station arrived at GameCo's company cabin, and Gordon Duffy led them through the woods to the grave. While one officer secured the site with yellow crime scene tape, his partner radioed the dispatcher to report a suspected homicide. The Sheriff's Department's Central Station serves a mixed bag of citizens and aliens in crowded urban areas, suburban developments, rural farmlands, and hordes of fun-and-sun-seeking tourists crowding mountain and river resort towns—plus the prospectors, military types, loners, cultists, survivalists, and kooks scattered about the county's cold, barren highlands and burning, low deserts.

The Big Bear dispatcher put in a request for a team of homicide investigators then called the county coroner's office to inform them that human remains had been found in a shallow grave in a ravine above Big Bear Lake.

Central Station dispatched Detectives Kelly Fahey and Luis

Torres to the scene, and put in a call to their team leader, Lieutenant Leonard Hicks, to inform him that two of his detectives were on their way to a homicide at Big Bear Lake.

When Hicks received the call, he was wrapping up a homicide investigation in Apple Valley, a small, desolate farming community a few miles east of Victorville in the Mojave Desert. He'd been roused from his bed at 4:00 in the morning to investigate the Apple Valley farmer who had been found in his pickup with a bullet in the head.

Hicks almost didn't respond to the Big Bear call after he booked the murder suspect at the Victor Valley jail. He was tired, and Saturday was supposed to be his day off, but Big Bear was one of the county's lowest crime areas. There hadn't been a murder there in four years; it was the county's most popular resort area, a Mecca for many prominent Los Angeles residents. Hicks knew the media wouldn't bat an eye if a body had been exhumed in a high crime area like San Bernardino or Fontana, but a murder at Big Bear could be big news in L.A., and he didn't want the media relations people on his back. So, when he pulled out of the Victor Valley jail parking lot in his GMC Yukon, he drove up the back side of Gold Mountain to Big Bear. He may have been covering his ass, but he rationalized that Big Bear really wasn't that far out of his way. Besides, he wanted to check in on Detectives Fahey and Torres, since they were both young and relatively inexperienced.

Fahey and Torres arrived at the crime scene, followed ten minutes later by the mobile crime lab and a coroner's van. Hicks finally arrived just over three hours after Gordon Duffy's 911 call. Hicks flashed his badge at the entrance to the property, and bounced the Yukon down the rutted trail through the woods to the gaggle of county vehicles scattered on a small clearing at the head of the ravine. Hicks grabbed his battered briefcase and clambered out of the SUV. After stretching his road-weary bones, he ducked his six-foot, three-inch frame under the yellow crime scene tape, and he followed the trail down the ravine to the grave where half a dozen detectives, crime lab technicians, and coroner's assistants were working.

Hicks found detective Kelly Fahey kneeling in the dirt next to the grave while Harry Smedley, an assistant coroner, examined the mound of muddy and moldering flesh that once had been a human being. Detective Luis Torres was videotaping the scene with a hand-held digital video camera.

"How's it going, Fahey?" Hicks asked.

"You kidding?" Fahey returned. "I hate my fucking job! How long does it take to get used to the stink?"

"You never do," he said, smiling down at her.

Fahey was a diminutive redhead in her late twenties, and for at least the hundredth time, Hicks thought she was the prettiest homicide detective he'd ever worked with. Of course, he'd never tell her that. He got down on his haunches beside her, breathing through his mouth, a trick he'd learned early in his career to reduce the stench of death. It really didn't work.

She'd been using a small digital audio recorder to dictate her notes. Switching it off, she looked up at him, returning his smile. "How was the Big Apple?" she asked, referring to his Apple Valley excursion.

"Rotten," he said.

"Just like our stiff," Torres quipped, still videotaping, with the broad, toothy grin of a man who loved to tease women. He was a wiry, cocky young man with permed black hair, an outstanding pair of ears and a pencil-thin mustache. When Torres took the Sheriff's Department physical, he had to drink half a gallon of water and stretch his skinny neck to its limits to pass the minimum weight and height requirements. Now, to look more macho, he wore snakeskin Mexican cowboy boots with three-inch heels and a Kevlar vest beneath his shirt, increasing his chest size two full inches. An illegal six-inch switchblade was invariably tucked into the top of his boot. None of this, however, compensated for his notoriously stale sense of humor.

"How long's he been in the ground, Harry?" Hicks asked the stout coroner's assistant who was huffing and puffing over the body.

"Four or five days. Maybe a week. Hard to say until the Bug Lady checks out the maggots," Smedley wheezed.

Hicks took a small, spiral-bound notebook and a ballpoint pen from his brief case. "Any idea what did him in?"

Smedley cleared the phlegm from his throat and spat it on the ground. "Well, there's a neat bullet hole above his left eye."

"But the shooter's motive definitely wasn't robbery." Fahey handed Hicks one of the plastic evidence bags she and Smedley had filled with the victim's personal effects.

Hicks gave the bag a cursory glance, but didn't open it, because he wasn't wearing gloves. "What's in the inventory?"

"The usual," Fahey said. "Credit card case and a money clip. Dead cell phone. Marlboros and a butane lighter. Then there's the not-so-usual. The guy was loaded. He had a gold Rolex calendar watch, gold chain, diamond pinky ring, and over two grand in the clip."

Hicks whistled and returned the bag to her. "Dealer?"

"Maybe. I kinda doubt it, though. Nothing on him to indicate it. Name on the driver's license is Samuel Shelton. Beverly Hills address."

Smedley handed Hicks another evidence bag. "We found this in his jacket pocket. Looks like a car door handle."

"That's about it." Fahey stripped off her latex gloves and brushed the dirt from the knees of her jeans. "Why would the guy be carrying a broken car door handle in his jacket pocket?"

"Maybe he wanted to get a handle on things," Torres said, zooming in for a close-up of her.

She flipped him the bird.

"How long will it take to finish here?" Hicks asked.

"Should be a wrap by dark," she replied.

"Once the remains are out of the hole, I want the site—"

"Gridded and gone over with a fine-tooth comb," Fahey finished for him. "I know, I know. Shit. We'll be here for a while."

"And keep those volunteers from the Big Bear station away from the site. They're here to secure the area, not to trample the evidence. Where's the couple who discovered the body?" Hicks asked.

"In their cabin down by the lake," Fahey said.

"Interview them yet?"

"Not really. Guy's cool, but she's really shook. Thought we'd wait and let you do it. Give her a little time to pull herself together."

6

Leonard Hicks peered through his spectacles at his spiral-bound notebook as he sat at the table in the kitchen of the Duffy's cabin, checking his notes. The rimless spectacles were new and expensive, and he hated that the so-called fashionable titanium springs needed constant adjusting. He absently took a sip from the mug of coffee Jen Duffy had heated up for him. It was tepid and weak, yet he took another sip, and looked up at her. She seemed to relax the more they talked. He thought she was very attractive; but then, he'd always been a sucker for English women. They sounded so intelligent.

"Good coffee, ma'am," he said with his most disarming smile. Hicks' wife had always claimed his smile and hands were his most endearing features. His smile, she told him, was just like Sean Connery's. He didn't believe it for a moment.

"Like a refill?" Jen Duffy asked.

"Thanks, but no. I'm just about through here." Hicks straightened in his chair, closed the notebook, slipping it into his coat pocket.

"Can I ask you a question, Lieutenant Hicks?" Gordon Duffy said.

"Fair enough."

"How long has the body been there?"

"Hard to say." Hicks rubbed the gray stubble on his chin. "The medical examiner will try to pinpoint the time of death, of course. The longer a body's been in the ground, the more difficult that is. The most accurate estimate will come from our forensic entomologist."

"You mean, an insect detective?" Jen asked.

Hicks smiled. She was bright. "We call her the Bug Lady. The larvae in and around the body are literally little time capsules."

Jen shivered. "Sounds like lovely work."

"Then you have no idea how long it's been out there?" Duffy asked.

"Just to guesstimate, I'd say a week, give or take a day or two."

Duffy seemed to relax. "My wife was afraid it happened last night while we were here."

Hicks shook his head. "Don't worry about that, ma'am. Victim's been in the ground a spell."

"Feel better?" Duffy asked her.

She still didn't look happy. "Not really, luv. The murder could've happened while you were up here last weekend."

Hicks pushed at his spectacles with his thumb and looked over them at Duffy. "You were here last week?"

Duffy nodded. "I came up Friday evening; got here about 7:30 and left Sunday afternoon around 4:00, I think."

"Anyone with you?"

"No, I was alone, working on a project all weekend."

"Did you hear any shots while you were here?"

"No, not that I remember. But I could have. There's nothing unusual about hearing shots up here."

"I know what you mean. We replace half the road signs every month or so. Damn kids use 'em for target practice." Hicks reached out to shake Jen's hand. "Well, I appreciate you folks helping us out. Sorry you had to find the body the way you did, ma'am."

32

Duffy and Jen walked him to the door.

"Then we can go back to L.A.?" Duffy asked.

"Don't see why not." Hicks smiled at Jen. "Thanks again for the cup of coffee, ma'am." He took out his card handed it to Duffy. "If you think of something you forgot to tell me, give me a call."

"We will," Duffy said.

Hicks started out the door. Jen stopped him with a touch on the arm. "You will find the murderer, won't you?"

"I'm sure we will, ma'am. Murders like this usually have a straight-line solution."

"Straight line?" Duffy asked.

Hicks explained, "When the perpetrator goes to all the trouble of burying a body, it usually indicates there's a direct link between the victim and the killer. Nine times out of ten, once we ID the victim, we make an arrest within twenty-four hours."

"You have no idea who the poor man was yet?" she said.

"Well, we do have a tentative ID." Hicks pulled out his notebook and thumbed through it. "According to his driver's license, his name was Samuel Shelton—"

"Oh, God, no!" she gasped.

Duffy paled. "Not Sam."

Hicks squinted at them. "You knew the deceased?"

Duffy shook his head, not comprehending. "We know Sam. He's our partner—"

"But it couldn't possibly be Sam," Jen interjected.

"Why's that, ma'am?"

Duffy said, "He's in Tokyo—"

"You know that for a fact, sir?"

"No, but he was booked on a flight out of LAX last Saturday night. I'm sure of that."

"Well, if that body out there's your partner, he never got to Tokyo," Hicks said.

"He's in Tokyo. I know he's in Tokyo," Duffy insisted.

"He never told you or anyone in your company about changing those plans?"

"That's not that unusual," Jen answered for her husband. "When Sam's out of the country he sometimes doesn't contact the office for a week or more. I mean, there's a seven-hour time difference between L.A. and Tokyo, and it's a day's difference. It's not easy to stay in contact by phone."

"What about e-mail?"

"Of course. We're in the electronics business," Duffy said. "But Sam's not your ordinary twenty-four-seven type of businessman."

She said, "Sam's a bit of a lone wolf. He actually enjoys being out of touch with the company. He looks upon business trips as a way of getting away from all the cares and pressures of the office."

"What's the name of your company?"

"GameCo."

"What type of business is it?"

"We design and market videogames."

"What's your position there?"

"I'm chairman and chief creative officer."

Hicks turned to Jen. "You also work there?"

"I head the design division."

"And what was Samuel Shelton's position?"

"President and chief financial officer."

"What was the reason for his trip to Tokyo?"

"A game fair," Duffy said. "One of our games—*Dead Rite*—won the Golden Gates Award for the best computer game of the year. Sam's there to accept the award for GameCo. Good God! It can't be Sam. I know he's in Tokyo."

Hicks closed his notebook. "Well, Mr. Duffy, there's one way to be sure, if you're willing."

7

Gordon Duffy stood on wobbly legs at the rear of the coroner's van, the nausea rising within him as he watched Harry Smedley and another assistant coroner slide a wire basket stretcher to the rear of the van. Hicks stood beside him, polishing the plastic lenses of his spectacles with his handkerchief. Hicks hooked the spectacles behind his ears, muttering, "Damn things cost over 300 dollars and I still can't see right." He blinked and looked down at the black body bag on the stretcher. "Well, let's see what we have here." He nodded at Smedley to unzip the bag. Torres turned on his video camera light. Hicks smiled at Duffy. "Hope you don't mind the camera. We've found it very helpful to tape every aspect of a homicide."

"It's your show," Duffy said.

Hicks opened his briefcase and took out a form. He handed the form and a pen to Duffy. "Sign this, please. It gives us the right to tape you."

The zipper on the body bag was stuck and Smedley wheezed and cursed, trying to jiggle it free.

"I want to warn you, Mr. Duffy, this won't be pleasant," Hicks said, putting the signed form back in his briefcase. "The victim was shot in the forehead and the body's been in the ground for quite some time."

Smedley continued to struggle with the zipper.

Hicks impatiently glanced at his watch. It was already after 4:00. "What's the problem, Harry?"

"Fucking zipper's shot," Smedley grumbled. "Goddamn bags are supposed to be disposable; but the coroner makes us reuse 'em. They sanitize 'em with steam and it rusts the fucking zippers."

Hicks said, "Let me try it, Harry." He reached past Smedley, pulled on the zipper, and it slid open easily, like its teeth had been sprayed with WD-40.

Hicks turned to Duffy. "Ready for this?"

"Let's get it over with."

Smedley turned back the flaps exposing the head of the victim. Duffy stared at the black and bloated face for a brief moment, rolled his eyes up and turned away, vomiting in the weeds next to the van. "It's Sam," he said.

"Sure?" Hicks asked.

"Yes, goddamn it! It's Sam! His front teeth were knocked out in a car accident a couple of years back. I recognize the bridgework."

Hicks nodded at Smedley. "Okay, Harry. Zip him up." He led Duffy away from the van and Torres started to follow with the video camera, but Hicks waved him off. "Cut, Torres. Get back to the site and help Fahey wrap it up." He thought Duffy still looked a little green. "Want to go back to your cabin? I've got more questions for you."

"Of course. Can we stay outside? I need some fresh air."

"Okay. But my back is killing me. It always does when I stand too much. Mind if we sit in my vehicle? We can keep the doors open."

They climbed into the Yukon, and Hicks seemed in no hurry to get down to business. He took out his notebook and thumbed through it for several minutes, giving Duffy time to regain his composure.

It was Duffy who finally broke the silence. "Sam wasn't exactly a lovable guy. But I don't know anyone who hated him enough to kill him."

"Hate usually has nothing to do with murder," Hicks said. "Would anyone profit from his death?"

Duffy sat there for a moment before he took a deep breath and answered, "No."

"You seem hesitant—"

"I was trying to think."

"Take your time."

"No. No one."

"How about you and your wife?"

"I can see how you might think that," Duffy said, "but Sam was our suit—"

"Suit?"

"He managed the company. Jen and I are creatives. Creative people need suits to handle the business details. We couldn't have built GameCo without Sam. He was indispensable. You don't kill indispensable people. Not unless you're nuts."

"Any next of kin?"

"He didn't have any. Not anyone close, anyway. At least, no one I know of."

"Was he married?"

Duffy shook his head. "Widowed. His wife, Mary, was an alcoholic. She drank herself to death four years ago."

"Never remarried?"

"No. He had an on-and-off again affair with Sharon Grant—"

"Sharon Grant? You mean, *the* Sharon Grant?"

"Yeah, the sitcom star. They met years ago."

"Before or after his wife died?"

"Way before. She was in a commercial we produced before we got into the game business."

"You said it was an on-again-off-again affair. Was it on or off?"

"Off. Sharon was supposed to go Tokyo with Sam, but they broke up a few days before they were scheduled to leave."

"Any idea why?"

"Booze. Shelton drank a lot. So did I before I gave it up. I'm a recovering alcoholic. It didn't seem to affect him. Some people can drink a lot without becoming alcoholics, but the women in his life couldn't seem to handle it. Like I said, his wife drank herself to death. Sharon had been hitting the bottle a lot, and she wanted to dry out, but she knew she couldn't as long as she was with Sam."

Hicks paused to scribble a few lines in his notebook, and then abruptly changed the subject. "When was the last time Shelton came up here?"

"Before last weekend, you mean?"

"Yes."

Duffy had to think. "About six months ago. Probably around the Fourth of July."

"Did he drive up alone?"

"No, Sharon was with him."

"That's Sharon Grant?"

"Yes."

"Think she drove him up here last weekend?"

"No way."

"His body was found on your property. There were no car keys in his personal effects. No abandoned vehicles have been reported in the vicinity, so I have to assume someone drove him up here."

"It wasn't Sharon."

"You seem positive of that."

"I am."

"Because you drove him up?"

"No."

Hicks changed the subject again. "Do you own a gun?"

Duffy didn't hesitate. "Yes. I collect them."

"I'd like to see your collection sometime."

"It's at my home in Bel Air. You're welcome to see it any time."

Hicks nodded but didn't say anything.

"You think I killed Sam, don't you?" Duffy finally said.

"I didn't say that. But to be honest, Mr. Duffy, you have to be considered a suspect. At this point, I've got to keep an open mind. Anyone who knew him could be considered a suspect." Hicks closed his notebook and slipped it into his briefcase.

Duffy asked, "So where do we go from here?"

"If I were you, I'd get back to L.A. I don't know enough yet to ask you any intelligent questions tonight, but I'll probably need to see you in my office sometime Monday morning."

"Monday?"

"Is that a problem?"

"No, not really."

"Okay. Take your wife and dog back to L.A. She's still very upset, and so are you. Tomorrow's Sunday—supposedly my day off—so tomorrow morning, I'm going to sit on my ass by the pool and read what the Sunday *L.A. Times* has to say about you and Shelton and the murder."

"You're releasing this to the media?"

"I'm not, but our media relations people will. Because Sharon Grant's involved, the media will dig up more about this case in a day than I could uncover in a week. So I'll let them do my spadework. You've got my card. That's my San Bernardino address. If you need to reach me before Monday, leave a message on my voice mail." Hicks shot Duffy a final glance. In his gut, he imagined Duffy losing his cool and making a run for it.

8

Except for one brief disagreement, Gordon and Jen Duffy hardly exchanged a word during their drive home. The disagreement was over their choice of radio stations. Their tastes were as far apart as their ages. Duffy wanted to listen to news radio to get the latest traffic reports, and to see if Shelton's murder had made the news. This bored Jen, and as soon as he tuned in, she waited a few minutes then switched to Viper Radio, which they listened to for the ride down the San Bernardino freeway to downtown L.A. Bob Dylan was singing *Just Like a Woman* when Duffy exited. Twisting through the maze of interchanges to the Harbor Freeway, he cut Dylan off by tuning back in to the news.

"I was listening to that," Jen complained.

He looked in the rearview mirror. "I want to see how the traffic is on the Santa Monica."

She let it go for the moment. "Is that car still following us?" she asked.

"What car?"

"The one you keep looking at in the rearview mirror."

He was surprised. "Am I that obvious?"

She turned and looked out the rear window. "Is it that green van behind us?"

"Yeah. I first noticed it about West Covina. But it could have followed us all the way from Big Bear."

"I doubt it."

"You think I'm a little paranoid?"

"More than a little. Why would anyone follow us?"

"Maybe Hicks put a tail on us."

She laughed. "Ridiculous. He knows we're going home."

They made the turn onto the Santa Monica Freeway, and Jen looked out the back window again. "You can stop worrying, luv. The van stayed on the freeway."

She switched back to Viper Radio. "Tell me something, luv," she said.

He gave her a sidelong glance. "What?"

"Did you kill Sam?"

Her question astonished him. "Jesus! Do you think I did?"

"Of course not."

"Then why ask?"

"Because you're acting so guilty. If you didn't kill Sam, you've nothing to worry about."

"Hicks thinks I did."

"My God! You do have a persecution complex, don't you?"

"Maybe he's playing mind games. Maybe he's smart. Maybe he thinks—"

"Maybe, maybe, maybe." Jen shook her head and laughed. "Maybe we should create a new game ... the *Maybe Game*. We could give people a million things to worry about. Now, please, luv. I don't want to talk about it."

She reached over and turned up the radio. Our Lady of Peace blared from the speakers as they turned onto the San Diego freeway and sped north five miles to the Sunset exit. Rufus, who had slept all the way from Big Bear, started whining intuitively the moment they turned off Sunset in Bel Air.

———

Two television remote vans and a knot of reporters, photographers, and TV news cameramen lay in wait for them by the entrance to their driveway. As Duffy turned in, reporters swarmed around the Navigator, pounding on the windows, shouting questions. Strobes flashed. Betacam lights blazed. Rufus leaped about the back of the van, clawing the windows and barking. An overeager TV news cameraman darted onto the driveway in their path. Duffy slammed on the brakes to avoid hitting him.

"Oh, God!" Jen gasped.

"Damn fools!" Duffy jammed the drive selector into reverse, turned his head, and tried to back down the driveway; but they were surrounded. He turned off the engine. "Shit," he muttered, giving Jen a helpless look. "What do we do now?"

"Grin and bear it, I suppose. We're bloody celebrities now."

Duffy couldn't tell by her smile if she was grinning and bearing it or simply enjoying it.

Someone yanked the driver's side door open; a rush of smoggy air and shouted questions poured in. Rufus scrambled over the seat and tried to jump out, but Duffy grabbed his collar and snapped on the leash. Rufus leaped out, almost yanking the leash from his hands. The reporters backed off, still shouting questions.

"Who killed Shelton?"

"Is that the dog that discovered the body?"

Jen climbed out her side and started around the front of the SUV. "Don't say anything," she warned Duffy.

"Did your husband kill his partner?" a woman shouted at her, thrusting a padded mike in her face.

Jen said nothing. She took Duffy's hand, and they ran for the house; Rufus led the way, barking and baring his fangs. The reporters let them pass, continuing their salvos of questions.

"What's Sharon Grant's involvement?"

"How'd you feel when you found the body?"

"Was Sharon Grant Shelton's lover?"

A photographer tried to block their way up the steps to the

front door, but Rufus lunged at him, jaws snapping, and he fell into the rose bushes. The lab and the Duffys bounded up the steps.

Their maid, Margarita, opened the door, frantically waving them inside, wailing, "Oh, Missus! Why are they here?"

"Mr. Shelton was murdered," Jen told her.

"Oh, no! Not Mr. Shelton!"

Duffy handed her the leash. "Take Mrs. Duffy and Rufus inside." He turned back to the reporters as they came up the steps behind him, shouted, "Sorry, we have nothing to say," and started to follow Jen into the house. The reporter who fell into the rose bushes leaped back onto the steps and tried to push his way in after them. Duffy shoved him back, bellowing, "Now wait a minute! Nobody gets into my house! Get the hell out of here!"

The photographer backed off, stumbling down the steps. Derisive laughter came from the newspeople crowding the sidewalk and lawn.

"What's the matter, Duffy?" one reporter taunted, "Afraid to answer a few questions?"

"If you didn't kill Shelton who did?" another yelled.

Their attitude infuriated him. Let them say what they wanted. He didn't give a damn. "That's all," he cut them off. "Any further statements will be made by my attorneys." He turned and stomped into the house, slamming the door behind him.

A woman bounded up the front steps, turned to her camera man, smiled ever so sweetly at the lens of his Betacam, and said, "Well, you heard it. Gordon Duffy refused to talk about the murder of his partner, Samuel Shelton, former lover of sitcom star Sharon Grant. That's all we have from the Duffy mansion in beautiful Bel Air. This is Liz Fujino returning you to the Channel Two Action Newsroom."

———

Duffy had slammed the door on the pandemonium outside only to find more of it inside the foyer of his twelve-room home. Rufus was leaping about the entrance hall, running in circles, madly barking, upsetting the umbrella stand by the door, slipping and sliding on the Persian scatter rugs. The doorbell chimed again and again, adding to the din and Rufus' excitement.

"Damn them!" Jen cried. "They have no right—"

Duffy shouted. "Rufus! Stop that!"

Margarita wailed, "They're driving him crazy!"

Duffy grabbed the Lab by the collar, snapped the leash back on and handed it to the maid. "Margarita, put him in his crate. Then fix us a pot of coffee and a sandwich or something light to eat. Bring them up to my study. Have Brandon fix the doorbells. Tell him I want to see him when he's finished."Duffy started up the stairs with Jen on his heels.

"What are we going to do, luv?"

"Well, first I'm going to my study to call George Crawford."

"George? Why George?"

"He *is* our attorney."

"But he's not a criminal lawyer."

"And I'm not a criminal."

"Gordon, please. You're a suspect. You need—"

He stopped at the door to his study and turned to her, placing his hands on her shoulders. "I need to talk to George. You need to take a soak in the Jacuzzi. This has been a hard day for us."

"You're right, of course," she appeased him. "But just a thought, luv. Remember the young attorney we met last summer when we went sailing on the Crawford's boat?"

He shook his head.

"I can't remember his name. But he was a criminal lawyer. George claimed he's very bright."

"Oh, yeah. George called him a young Barry Scheck."

"Well? Ask George about him. Even if you aren't a criminal." She gave him a peck on the cheek and headed down the hall toward the master bedroom.

He closed the door, went to the gun cabinet on the far wall and stood there a moment, staring through its glass doors at the weapons inside. Then he crossed to his desk, sank down in his leather executive chair, took out his cell phone, found a number in its phone book, and punched the talk button. It rang six times before a woman's voice answered. "It's me," he said softly.

"Who the fuck're you, Mr. Me?"

"Me, Gordon—"

"Oh, yeah, Gordon. Wunnerful old friend, you know something? I loved that old bastard. He left his fucking wife for me ... and now someone's killed him. He's dead ... I'm dead, and my whole fucking world's dead."

"Sharon, I'm sorry—"

"You're dead, too, Gordon, only you don't know it ... and I don't like talking to dead people."

"Sharon, listen —"

"Fuck you!"

Duffy heard a dial tone, and then a knock on the study door.

"Come in," he said.

Margarita opened the door, flashed him a nervous smile, and carried a tray with a coffee carafe and two sandwiches: corned beef for him and watercress for his wife. He took his sandwich from the tray. "Mrs. Duffy's in the Jacuzzi. Leave the tray for her in our bedroom."

"Yes, okay. Brandon says he'll have the doorbells fixed in a jiffy. I told him to come up here when he's finished."

"Thanks, Margarita. Oh, and no more calls tonight. Understand?"

A few minutes later, Brandon Cash entered Duffy's study. A tall, earnest young man, he was part-time bartender, part-time handyman, full-time law student at UCLA. He paid for his room and board at the Duffys by doing odd jobs whenever they had something that needed fixing.

"You wanted to see me?" Cash asked.

"How come you're not with Sharon?"

46

"She seemed okay this afternoon. I have an article to write for the *Law Review*—"

"Don't you know what happened?"

"You mean to Mr. Shelton? Margarita told me he'd been murdered when she asked me to fix the doorbells."

"That's the first you heard about it?"

"Yeah."

"Didn't you wonder what all those media people were doing here?"

"I had my headphones on, and I told Margarita I had a lot of studying to do. So, she never came out back to tell me anyone was bothering her."

"Well, now you know. And so does Sharon. I just talked to her. She's taking it pretty hard—"

"She crocked?"

Duffy nodded. "You'd better get over there."

"You coming later?"

"Not tonight. Stay with her until morning."

"No problem."

"Oh, and ride your bike. It's only a few blocks, but I don't want any of those news hounds following you."

"They won't. Anything else?"

"I'll be over first thing in the morning. Have her sober by then."

9

Leonard Hicks returned to his office at 7:30 that evening and called the medical examiner's office to see if an autopsy had been scheduled for Samuel Shelton. Dr. Charles Giese, the San Bernardino county deputy medical examiner answered. He was working late, catching up on his autopsy reports.

"Sorry, Len, the Shelton stiff isn't here yet. Can't schedule anything until it's been checked in," Dr. Giese told him. "You in a hurry on this one?"

"No more than usual. But I'd like to be an observer."

"Can't schedule anything tonight. How about tomorrow?"

"The later the better. I'm dead tired. Been up since 4:00 a.m."

Hicks hung up, reached into the bottom drawer of his desk, and took out the toilet kit and clean shirt he always kept there for emergencies. A hot shower would wash away the dust of the desert and the sweat he'd worked up tromping through the woods at Big Bear. Fifteen minutes later, he emerged from the men's locker room smelling of aftershave, not quite feeling like a new man, but better. Fahey and Torres were waiting for him in his office. She was glancing through a copy of *People*; he was cleaning his fingernails with a switchblade knife.

Hicks said, "That pig sticker's illegal, Torres."

Torres shrugged as if he had heard that a thousand times, closed the blade and slipped the knife into his boot.

"What's on our menu for tomorrow?" Fahey asked.

"Hate to ask you guys to put in another weekend," Hicks said, "but I'd like you two to drive down to Beverly Hills. Check out Shelton's high-class condo. There may be doormen or garage attendants you can interview. See if you can con someone into letting you into his apartment.

"Without a warrant?" Torres asked.

"It's just a fishing expedition. Don't tear the place apart."

"Okay," Fahey said. "Anything else?"

"If you have time, try to set up an interview with Sharon Grant. Shelton had a long-time affair with her. She could be a big help if she's willing to cooperate."

"Hey, let's put her on the suspect list. I'd love to grill her," Torres slurped.

Hicks ignored him. "Where's that car door handle that was found on the body?" he asked Fahey.

She patted her evidence case. "Right here."

"Get it up to latent prints. When they're finished with it, see if the crime lab can come up with the make and model of the vehicle it came from."

"Will do," she said.

"And how do you plan to spend your Sunday?" Torres asked.

"Going to sleep all morning. Then I'm observing Shelton's autopsy at 2:30."

"He gets all the perks," Fahey said.

———

About the time Hicks arrived home, Brandon Cash turned his mountain bike into the driveway of a white brick ranch house on Bellagio Road in Bel Air. Geoffrey Seaman, the film director, whom Cash only knew because he was Gordon Duffy's friend and AA sponsor, owned the house. Seaman was in Ireland for three months shooting a film; Duffy had arranged for Sharon Grant to stay at his home while she dried out.

Cash walked his bike through the perfume of night-blooming jasmine to the side door by the kitchen. He locked the bike to a breezeway post and went up the steps to the kitchen door. He unlocked the door and entered the house, and a spicy incense and the unmistakable odor of cannabis replaced the sweet perfume outside. The twangy defiance of the Eagles' *Already Gone* blared from the media room as he entered the code to turn off the security system. He headed for the sound and flipped on a light switch, bathing the media room in bright, Halogen lights from spots recessed into the ceiling.

Sharon Grant groaned and threw her arm over her eyes. She squinted up at Cash; and when she recognized him, mumbled, "Oh, shit, Brandon. Trying to fucking save me?"

The star of the *Sharon Grant Show* was sprawled out on the distressed leather couch like a broken marionette. To her fans, and there were tens of millions of them, Sharon would always be a bright, vibrant Greenpeace lobbyist living in sin with a wacky, young Congressman from the religious right. Cash turned off the stereo, crossed to the couch, and saw her for what she was: a sad, fucked up woman. Her strawberry blond hair was a mat of plastered, greasy strings; her normally pink and freckled face had a sickly, gray pallor; perspiration glistened on her brow; and her skin smelled like she'd been swimming in a vat of scotch. He took her wrist to feel her pulse, and she stirred at his touch. Clear vomit ran down her chin and neck, staining her creamy silk lounging pajamas.

"Oh, God," the star moaned. "I wanna die, Brandon ..."

"That's obvious." He lifted the almost empty liter of Cutty Sark from the coffee table and shook it at her. "Drink all this tonight?"

She rolled over on her side, away from him and the light. "Go 'way. Please, I don't need you. I don't want you. Go home. Get the fuck out of my life!"

"How much did you drink?"

"Just a few shots ... really kiddo. I'll swear to God, if that helps."

"And what did you smoke?"

"Don't fuck with me! I'm in fucking pain!"

"Wrong, you *are* a fucking pain." He sat on the couch next to her, and she didn't resist when he gently rolled her onto her back. Her top three buttons were undone, exposing one of her breasts. He buttoned her up, thinking she had a nice rack for a woman in her forties. When he pried open an eyelid and looked into her pupils, he didn't like the dilation he saw one damn bit.

"What else did you take?"

She sniffed to clear the vomit from her nose. "Nothing, dammit you ... leave me alone, kid. You shouldn't see me this way. No one should ... I just wanna die ..."

"Snort a little coke?"

"No ... no ... I don't do coke."

"Since when?"

"Since I gave it up, you stupid fuck!"

"Smoke a little rock?"

"Just a little grass." Her head lolled from side to side as she wiped the drool from her chin with the back of her hand. "I swear to God, so help me ..."

"Pop any pills?"

"No, that fucking Duffy flushed 'em."

Cash got up from the couch and headed for the kitchen, taking the bottle of Cutty with him.

"Sam's dead ... you know that?" she shouted after him. "Sam's dead!"

Brandon bit his lip as he poured what was left of the scotch down the drain, then returned to the couch with a dish towel and a pan of ice water.

Sharon was ranting to herself. "Oh, Sam! My poor Sam ... I should've been with you."

"Be glad the asshole's dead."

"You little shit!" she spat.

He began to wipe the vomit from her chin and neck. "Whatever."

"Brandon," she asked, "Did you kill Sam?"

"Where'd you get the Cutty?"

"People next door. I told them I ran out ... I really needed it."

"They give you the grass, too?"

She shook her head. "No, bought it. A whole lid. That kid who delivers papers. He's great, huh?"

"Yeah, great."

"So? I slipped a little. Sam's dead, you fuck!"

"And you'll join him if you don't lay off the booze and dope."

Sharon started to cry. "I wanna die. Don't you understand, kiddo? I wanna die." Her sobs were interrupted by a coughing fit, and she passed out.

Brandon lifted her surprisingly light frame from the couch, carried her into the master bedroom, and laid her down gently on the California-king bed, covering her with a comforter. For more than a few minutes, he stood by her feeling her pulse, listening to her breathing. Satisfied that her heart wasn't going to stop, he sat on the Kennedy rocker next to the bed, and stretched out the best he could. He knew it was going to be a long night.

An alcoholic and addict himself since he was in his teens, Brandon was not without compassion. He sat watch for hours, holding her right hand. Gradually, her breathing became more regular and she slept soundly. A little before midnight, he snapped on the bedside light and saw that the pink had returned to her cheeks. She'd thrown off the comforter in her sleep, so he reached across her body to pull it back, brushing her breast with his forearm as he did. She stirred at his touch, and it gave him a quick rush. He turned out the light, hoping he hadn't disturbed her, leaned back in the rocker, closed his eyes, and relaxed for the first time since he entered the house. He wished he could crawl into bed next to her. She could be such a beautiful person when she wasn't drinking. The thought made him glad, again, that Shelton was dead.

———

Jen was at her dressing table, brushing out her long auburn hair, clad only in bikini panties. In the mirror, her eyes followed Duffy as he crossed the room with a small, worried frown on his face. Kissing her on the back of the neck, he whispered, "God, you smell good."

"Did you call George?"

"Mmm." He went into his walk-in closet.

"What did he say?"

"That I could be in one hell of a mess." Coming out of the closet in his undershorts, he sat down on the edge of the bed and took off his socks.

"Did you ask him about that young attorney?"

"Uh, huh. Guy's name is Baldwin ... Matt Baldwin. I'm meeting with them tomorrow afternoon."

She picked up a bottle of lotion and began creaming her legs.

"Good. Now you can stop worrying and relax."

"That was George's advice, too." Duffy lay down on the bed, clasping his hands behind his head on the pillow. After a long moment, he said, "Christ, Jen, I didn't kill Sam."

10

It was light outside when Brandon Cash's eyes flickered and opened. He glanced at his watch and saw it was nearly 9:00. Sharon Grant was also awake, curled on her side, staring at him through swollen, half-closed lids, the trace of a smile on her crusty lips. "Been here all night, kiddo?" she croaked.

"Yeah." He rubbed the sleep out of his eyes. "How do you feel?"

"Shitty."

He got up from the rocker, feeling like shit himself. "I'll get some aspirin."

"Nah, I'll get it. I have to pee anyway." She sat up and tried to get out of bed, but got no further than the sitting position. "Oh, God, my head!"

"Sure you don't want me to get the aspirin?"

"You wanna take a leak for me, too? Just shut up and make some coffee."

She managed to climb out of bed and padded past him, heading toward the bathroom, holding her temples.

"Was it worth it?"

She looked back at him over her shoulder, pained in more ways than one. "Fuck off, Brandon."

"Getting drunk never solves anything."

"Just start the coffee, man. I really can't handle your sanctimonious bullshit this morning."

"It's not bullshit."

"Bullshit," she said, disappearing into the bathroom and slamming the door behind her.

Cash went to the kitchen. He was filling the coffeepot at the sink when he saw Duffy's Mercedes pull into the driveway. He unlocked the kitchen door, poured the water into the coffeemaker, and Duffy came in carrying a copy of the *L. A. Sunday Times*.

"How is she?" he asked.

"Hung over in the bathroom. I'm making coffee."

"We may have to send her to The Betty Ford Center if she can't hack this on her own."

"Mr. Shelton's murder really has her shook. Give her a few more days. If it's okay with you, I'll pick up my stuff and stay here."

"Only if you think you're up to it."

Duffy put the *Times* down on the counter. "You look like hell."

"I slept most of the time ... in a rocking chair. I'm a little stiff, that's all."

"I'll take her the coffee. Go home and get your stuff." He tossed him his car keys. "I'll watch her until you get back."

"Anything in the paper about Mr. Shelton?"

"It's all over the front page."

"I shouldn't say it, but I'm glad the asshole's dead."

"Yeah? Well, keep thoughts like that to yourself, Brandon."

"Okay. But it's true."

Duffy poured himself a cup of coffee. "You realize the police may question you."

"Me? Why?"

"Because I'm probably a suspect."

"That's crazy."

"Maybe. But I was at the cabin ... alone ... all weekend."

"*All* weekend?"

Duffy nodded. "Yes. And you spent the entire weekend here with Sharon. You were afraid to leave her alone."

Cash shook his head. "I don't know, Mr. Duffy. If I'm learning nothing else in law school, it's that once people start lying, everything screws up—"

"You were with her, weren't you?"

"Yes, but—"

"Then just say the two of you were here all weekend."

"What if she won't back me up?"

"She will. I'll see to that."

"Mr. Duffy, I still don't like this."

"Look, I'm not asking you to lie, Brandon," Duffy said, getting flustered. "But in the real world, sometimes we have to stretch the truth a bit. I'm surprised they haven't taught you that in law school yet."

"I think I know why you're doing this, I'm just not sure you're right. If I were your lawyer—"

"Yeah, well, let me handle my defense."

———

Duffy and Sharon Grant had coffee in the sunspace off the kitchen. She looked like a wraith as she sat there, clad in a wispy black silk dressing gown, peering at the front page of the paper. She raised her red-rimmed eyes to him and he shifted uneasily in his chair.

"You're unbelievable, Duffy. Sam's dead, and all you give a shit about is your fucking wife."

"I'm always here when you need me."

"You screw up my life, and you want me to believe you're helping me?"

"Sam screwed up your life."

"Leave him out of this, goddamn it!"

"All I'm asking is that you tell the police you spent the weekend here with Brandon."

"And have my fans think I shacked up with a handyman young enough to be my kid? No fucking way."

"Do you want the truth to come out?"

"Are you kidding? My whole life's been a lie."

"Then help me. I don't want Jen—"

"Hello? I don't give a damn about Jen! I can't handle any more bullshit. You know how fucked up I've been. Sometimes I don't know what's the truth and what isn't. And I can't remember a god-damn thing anymore. If I start lying—"

"All you have to remember is that Brandon spent the weekend here with you."

"I need a fucking drink."

"Fine. Have a drink. And when Brandon gets back we'll drive you to Betty Ford—"

She let out a sigh of resignation. "Shit. Okay. I'll say whatever you want me to say."

11

A little after 11:00 Sunday morning, Fahey and Torres arrived at Sam Shelton's condo in Beverly Hills on Avenue of the Stars just north of Pico. They parked their unmarked car in the outdoor visitor's lot above the building's underground garage. After they identified themselves to the doorman on duty, Torres took the elevator down to the underground garage to question the attendants. Fahey interviewed the doorman in the lobby.

"Were you on duty last weekend?" she asked, her microrecorder in his face.

"Yeah. I'm the daytime duty man for weekends."

"Then you were on duty that Saturday?"

He nodded. "Every Saturday and Sunday. Seven in the mornin' to 7:00 at night. Johnny Meikle takes over from 7:00 p.m. to 7:00 a.m."

"You always work a twelve-hour day?"

"You get full benefits if you work at least twenty-four hours a week. We also fill in for the weekday guys if they need a rest."

"And you check everyone in and out of the building?"

"No one gets past me."

"Can they enter through the garage?"

"Only if they drive in. But if a car don't have no building sticker, the garage guys send 'em back up to the visitors' lot. They still gotta get by me."

"Do you know the residents by sight?"

"Most of 'em."

"Samuel Shelton?"

"Sure. He was one of our original owners."

"Do you remember if Mr. Shelton entered or left the building while you were on duty a week ago yesterday?"

"A week ago Saturday? No ... but then, Mr. Shelton wasn't much of a walker. Always entered and left through the garage. About the only time I ever saw him was when he'd come down to get his mail."

"You see him pick up his mail that Saturday?"

He scratched his chin. "A week's a long time to remember people comin' or goin' or pickin' up mail. But if he did, I seen him."

"Recall if he had any guests that Saturday?"

"No, but let's check the log book..." The doorman went to his desk, pulled out a large ledger from the center drawer and flipped through it. "It's a shame about Mr. Shelton. Can't say I really knew him. He wasn't very friendly. But he musta had something—money, I suppose. Women seemed to have a thing for him." He winked at her. "And some of 'em were pretty famous."

"Like Sharon Grant?"

"I thought so, but she hasn't been around for a while. They were pretty hot and heavy up to a few weeks ago." He found the page with the entries for January tenth. "Let's see, here." He ran his finger down the page. "Nope, Mr. Shelton didn't have no guests that day. Just a drugstore boy that delivered a prescription for him. Checked him in at 5:45 Saturday and out at 5:52."

"Was Mr. Shelton in his apartment at the time?"

"Yep, he was in all right. I don't let anyone in 'less I check with the resident first over the intercom."

"Has anyone else been up to Mr. Shelton's apartment at anytime during the last week?" Fahey asked, peering over the guest book.

The doorman slowly paged through the register. He finally closed the book and said, "Nope, not a one."

"Is there a copy machine in the building? I'd like a copy of all the entries in your guest registry for the past month."

"I guess I could do that. There's one in the office."

"Do you have a key to Mr. Shelton's apartment?"

"Yes, ma'am. Got keys to all the apartments, for emergencies, you know."

"I'd like to get that key, if I could." Fahey tried to sound as matter-of-fact as possible.

"Uh, I don't know, ma'am."

"This is a *police* emergency. Mr. Shelton was murdered, and my partner and I have to examine his residence." Fahey saw that the doorman was trying to cover his ass, so she went for the throat. "I shouldn't tell you this, but Sharon Grant hasn't been seen for over a week. Her body could be up there." Fahey nodded seriously.

The doorman led her into his cubbyhole of an office, took a ring of keys from his belt; and opened the cabinet where the keys to all the apartments were hanging from hooks. He took down the one tagged 21C, saying, "I appreciate you don't tell nobody I gave you this."

———

Down in the garage, Torres was talking to one of the attendants, a huge man in blue coveralls with *Harry* embroidered over the left breast pocket.

"Yeah. I remember Mr. Shelton leaving here that night," Harry was saying. "He roars out of here in that green Jag of his 'bout 7:00, maybe 7:30—"

"Sure it was a week ago Saturday night?" Torres asked.

"You bet your ass. I wasn't on duty that night."

"Then how could you remember?"

"Easy, man. That's why I remember. I pick up a few extra bucks when I'm off-duty, chauffeurin' residents to or from LAX ... stuff like that. I was supposed to take Mr. Shelton to the airport at 7:00 that night. The man don't like to leave his Jag at LAX—"

"Can't say I blame him."

"You better believe it, man. So I got here 'bout quarter to 7:00—I always like to be a little early—and while I was waitin' for Mr. Shelton to come down, I stood around shootin' the shit with Amos, one of the regular Saturday night duty guys. 'Bout five to 7:00, Shelton calls down and tells me he's cancelin' his trip. But he told me to wait; says he'll pay me just the same. Real nice, right? Anyways, the man's real shook when he comes down to pay me my fifty bucks. Tells me he has to drive to San Bernardino 'cause his partner's been in an accident—"

"His partner? You sure he said that, Harry?"

"Yeah, man. That's what the man say. Accident in San Bernardino. My cousin lives out there. That's how I remember."

———

Fahey and Torres took the elevator up to Shelton's apartment. "How'd you get that old guy to give you the key without a warrant?" Torres asked.

"I beat it out of him."

"Lucky guy," Torres said, licking his lips at Fahey, who ignored him.

They pulled on latex gloves and entered Shelton's apartment. Torres let out a low whistle when they got inside. "Damn!"

"No shit! I'd kill for a place like this." Fahey crossed the living room to the sliding glass doors that opened onto the balcony. "What a view! You can see the fucking Santa Monica pier!"

"Shelton sure was a neat freak," Torres said from the living room. "Looks like the clean room at Intel."

Fahey turned away from the windows. "It's got sort of a limbo feel."

"Limbo?" Torres danced, rattling his scrawny shoulders and hips.

"The place between heaven and hell where they send kids who die before they're baptized. Everything's white-on-white, like living on a cloud."

"Sounds cool."

"Yeah, but you gotta be dead to get there." She crossed to the doorway of the master bedroom suite. "What a fucking bed! Super-king size ... uh-oh, looks like Shelton never finished packing." Fahey slid the half-packed suitcase across the bed and sat down, checking out the room. "What a freak! The ceiling's all mirrors. You could watch yourself fucking."

Torres bound into the room. "Hey, Red. I just got a great idea."

"Fuck off. All you'll ever get from me is a mouthful of knuckles."

Torres sat on the bed. "Caller ID light's blinking on his phone."

"Well don't touch it. This is just a fishing expedition. We don't have a warrant."

"Who'll know?" Torres lifted the cordless phone on the bedside table and pressed the CID button. "Last call came in at 6:11 p.m. January ten. That's only half an hour before the garage guy says Shelton left for San Bernardino."

"So, who called?"

"Display says it's an unknown name and number."

"Great. And there haven't been any other calls for over a week?"

"Anyone who knew Shelton probably thought he was out of the country. Or he may have a system that screens unwanted calls."

"Any other calls that day?"

Torres touched the review button. "One from Thrifty Drugs at 4:47, and just two others; both GameCo numbers, one at 2:22, the other at 11:46. That's it for January ten."

"Guess he wasn't a very popular guy. But you'd better leave it; we can get all his records from the phone company."

"Mmm-hmm. Hold on." Torres pressed the redial button and the phone on the other end of the line rang twice before a woman answered.

"Sorry to bother you ma'am. This is Detective Torres. I'm with the San Bernardino Sheriff's Department—"

"Oh, yes. I've been expecting one of you."

"That a fact, ma'am?"

"I'm Virginia Reed, Mr. Shelton's executive assistant."

Torres put his hand over the phone's mouthpiece and whispered to Fahey, "She's Shelton's secretary."

"See if she'll talk to us."

Torres uncovered the mouthpiece. "Ah, ma'am, my partner and I are in the neighborhood. Can we drop by this afternoon and ask you a few questions?"

"Of course." She gave Torres her address in Brentwood, then added, "I'll be home the rest of the day."

After Torres hung up, he noticed the note pad next to the phone. Examining it closer, he saw it had an impression on the top blank sheet made by a ballpoint pen. "Hey, look at this," he said, handing the pad to Fahey.

"It's too faint to read."

"We could sprinkle some police fairy dust on it."

"Dumbass. I don't want to ruin it before the crime lab checks it out."

"Thought we didn't have a warrant," Torres whined.

Fahey carefully slipped it into a plastic evidence bag. "So arrest me."

12

Gordon Duffy's meeting with his attorneys took place at 1:00 p.m. in the plush Beverly Hills law offices of Crawford, Raskin, Lutz, and Baldwin. George Crawford, the firm's scholarly, white-maned senior partner, sat in for a few minutes, just long enough to introduce Duffy to Matthew Baldwin. He then excused himself, stating that criminal law was not his bailiwick, and apologizing profusely that he had another commitment, which from his casual attire and the fact that it was Sunday, Duffy guessed was a golf date.

Duffy considered himself a self-made man, and as such, he never really trusted the professional class. To his way of thinking, most medical doctors were modern-day fakirs, plumbers of the body; accountants were boring idiot savants who reduced every-thing to the bottom line; teachers—especially college professors—were overeducated fools who couldn't make it in the real world. And lawyers stood on the lowest rung of his professional ladder—he considered them legal prostitutes who would climb into bed with any murderer, thief, or cheat if the price was right.

Baldwin didn't seem to fit Duffy's mental image of a lawyer. He was tall and thin and had a full head of black hair. Round, horn-rimmed glasses couldn't hide the twinkle in his eyes, and they gave him an intelligent, sincere look. His style of dress was California-layered: loose, brown suede vest over a pale green linen shirt, over a white t-shirt tucked into black cargo pants. On a more delicate man, the look might have seemed too boyish. On Baldwin, it only emphasized his masculine good looks. He appeared completely at ease as he sat in his leather executive chair, his size thirteen Mephisto loafers propped up on his desk, a yellow legal pad on his lap.

It didn't take long for Duffy to decide he liked the man. Baldwin was a different breed of professional—a creative lawyer—and an empathetic bond was established between them in his mind.

"Well, what do you think?" Duffy asked after he'd finished his recitation of the facts, as he knew them.

"Frankly, from what you've told me, I'd say your biggest problem is the stock agreement. It gives you a motive."

"You think I'll be indicted?"

"If the DA assigns an ambitious prosecutor to the case, he might indict to grab some headlines. I suppose he could dig up enough circumstantial evidence to make it through a preliminary hearing. But to convict? Not a chance. Not if you don't make any more mistakes. For example, you never should have agreed to meet Hicks at his office tomorrow morning."

"That was a mistake?"

"Tactical error. One of the first rules of this game is never agree to meet the opposition on his turf. It gives him the home field advantage."

"I wasn't aware this was a game."

"Now you are. It's a far more intricate and dangerous game than the ones you dream up. There's only one way to play it: to win."

"You'd defend me even if you thought I was guilty?"

"Your guilt or innocence isn't my concern. It's up to the police and the DA's office to determine if they have enough evidence to indict. Only a court of law is entitled to judge you."

"I didn't kill Sam."

"I believe you. Feel better?"

Duffy nodded.

"Okay. Let's do a little situational analysis." Baldwin leaned back in his chair, clasping his hands behind his head. "I don't expect you to be indicted, but we don't know how much evidence Hicks has, or if there are other suspects. There's always the chance that you'll be brought to trial, so everything we do, we do as if we're going to end up playing it to a jury. Got it?"

"You're the boss. Tell me how to play it."

"Start thinking of Hicks as the enemy. Detectives are trained to interpret a suspect's emotional state, and you've been giving off guilty signals."

"How do you mean?"

"If a man with your money and power were innocent, he'd act indignant if he were asked to drive all the way to San Bernardino just to answer a few questions." He turned to his computer screen, and clicked open his address book. "I went to law school with a guy who's a prosecutor in the San Bernardino County DA's office. Joe Walker. Let's see if we can move your meeting with Hicks tomorrow to our turf." He clicked Walker's name, and the computer dialed the number.

Duffy soaked in Baldwin's Hollywood ego, and he considered it another plus. Baldwin cradled the receiver under his chin as he waited for someone to answer his call.

"Hello," he sang. "Is your daddy there?" He winked at Duffy and doodled on his legal pad as he waited for Walker to come on the line. "Joe? Matt Baldwin." He nodded several times. "Sure has been a long time. How's Jill?" More nodding. "Another one on the way? No kidding." He grinned and shook his head. "No, haven't married yet. Having too much fun as a bachelor." After a series of uh huhs, he finally got to the point. "Say, I know it's Sunday, Joe, and I hate screwing up your day off, but I really called to ask if the Shelton case has been assigned to anyone in your office yet." He nodded again and gave Duffy thumbs up. "You think you've got it? Good. Then I have a small complaint." Another pause. "No, nothing serious. I represent Gordon Duffy. More doodling. "Yeah, that's the guy. Seems one of your homicide dicks wants my client to drive all the way to San Bernardino tomorrow morning for an interview. Name's Hicks. Know the guy?" Pause. "Oh, *Lieutenant* Hicks, is it? Well, I don't give a damn if he's General Hicks. He has no right to waste my client's time like that." Pause. "No, I don't object to Duffy being interviewed, but Hicks can't expect him to drive all that way just to chat. My client's the chairman of a major software company. He's busy as hell, and so am I. Unless Hicks plans to book my client, the meeting will be in my office, not his. You can arrange that, can't you, old buddy?" He listened for a moment. "How about 10:00 tomorrow morning?" His smile broadened. "Great! Thanks, Joe. I owe you one. Give Jill my love."

The smile disappeared from Baldwin's face the second he hung up. "Walker's been assigned the case."

"That's good, isn't it? You said he's an old friend."

"There are no friendships in this business. I'd say you've got a damn good chance of being indicted. Joe's a very competitive guy. Ambitious as hell. There's nothing he'd rather do than meet me in court."

13

It was a beautiful Sunday afternoon in Southern California. An hour before Samuel Shelton's autopsy, Hicks was sunning his weary bones by the pool of his four bedroom stucco pseudo-Spanish tract home in Loma Linda when his cell phone rang. He hoped it was his wife, Honey, calling to say she was finally coming home. She'd been visiting their daughter in Connecticut for over a week after the birth of their first grandchild. He eagerly flipped his cell open and was disappointed. The caller ID said it was Joe Walker, an Assistant DA in the county prosecutor's office.

"What can I do for you, Joe?" Hicks answered.

"A little bird told me you're planning to interview Gordon Duffy in your office tomorrow morning about the Shelton case?"

"Got a problem with that?"

"I don't. But Duffy's attorney does. He'd prefer to have the meeting in his Beverly Hills office."

"Duffy has an attorney?"

"One of the hottest defense attorneys in L.A. Of course, if you have enough evidence to book Duffy, you can still demand they meet you out here."

"You know I don't. I'm still waiting for the results of the autopsy this afternoon. Until I get them, Duffy's not an official suspect. But if he's hired a defense attorney he must be worried about something."

"Not necessarily. He just may not like the idea of wasting a day driving out here. Can't say I blame him. He's probably a very busy guy."

"So, he wants to waste my day?"

"I'm sure his attorney's calling the shots. It's Matthew Baldwin, a rising star at Crawford, Ruskin, Lutz, and Baldwin in Beverly Hills. The firm's got a great reputation. Mostly corporate stuff. Baldwin heads their criminal law department."

"He good?"

"You ought to know. You were a witness on one of the cases he defended. State of California versus Raymond Keller. Remember the case?"

"How could I forget? Keller was the L.A. skin photographer who screwed his models, then hacked them to bits and scattered the pieces all over the Mojave for the coyotes to eat. Baldwin's the asshole who got him off?"

"Led the defense team. You're right about the asshole bit. Real asshole and real expensive. He's sort of a celebrity now and gets a lot of press; the media built his reputation. In my book, he's way overrated. Baldwin was a year ahead of me at Boalt Hall. I always thought he was just another pretty boy smartass jerk."

"What time does he want to meet with Duffy and me?"

"Ten a.m. sharp."

"So, I have to fight rush hour traffic all the way to Beverly Hills?"

"Like I said, you can always cancel."

"No way. Tell the asshole I'll be there."

––––––

Detectives Torres and Fahey arrived at the Brentwood apartment of Virginia Reed shortly after 2:00 that afternoon. The first thing

Samuel Shelton's executive assistant said after they identified themselves at her front door was, "If you ask me, Gordon Duffy deserves a kiss."

Her remark surprised Fahey. "Oh, why's that, ma'am?" she asked as they were led to the living room.

Ms. Reed motioned for them to sit on the couch. "Isn't it obvious?" she said.

"We try to keep an open mind about these things," Torres said as he and Fahey sat.

Fahey took out her micro-recorder and held it up for the woman to see. "Mind if I record our conversation, ma'am?"

"Not at all. Mr. Shelton was a hateful man. He had absolutely no respect for women. He was a groper, you know."

"Really?" Fahey said. "I hate those grab-ass guys."

Ms. Reed nodded her head in agreement. "And he had a toilet mouth. He said and did the most demeaning things to women. He murdered his wife, you know."

Ms. Reed was not quite old enough to be Fahey's grandmother, but she wondered if the woman was a little batty or suffering delusions from the shock of her boss's murder.

"No, we haven't heard that one." Torres said. "What makes you think he murdered his wife?"

"Oh, I know he did. Well, not in a legal sense, maybe. But he played around with younger women."

Torres said, "Lots of men do that. It doesn't make them murderers."

"Oh, I know that. But it still doesn't make it right. What's this country coming to?"

"Men just aren't what they used to be," Fahey said, throwing Torres a deadpan look.

Ms. Reed cleared her throat and continued. "Mr. Shelton had a strange metabolic disorder. Sort of a reverse diabetes. Alcohol didn't make him drunk, it simply gave him more energy the same way uppers give ordinary people energy."

Torres and Fahey exchanged glances and he said, "I'm not really following you."

"Mr. Shelton used alcohol as a weapon. He murdered his wife, Mary, with it. And he was killing Sharon with it—"

"That's Sharon Grant?" Fahey asked.

"Yes. A wonderful actress. Very talented. At least, she was before Sam turned her into a drunk. Sharon was one of the original GameCo backers, you know."

Fahey and Torres nodded, letting the woman chat away.

"Mr. Shelton and Gordon were originally in the commercial film business. Hodgepodge Productions. Their studio actually gave Sharon her first film job, a part in a cola commercial. Anyway, by the 80s, she was a star, and Hodgepodge was getting into more computer animation and special effects. It was only natural to move into the video game business. Sharon put up a quarter of a million dollars to keep GameCo going in the early days."

Torres whistled. "That's a lot of lettuce."

Ms. Reed waved it off as if his remark were a gnat. "Peanuts compared to what the company's worth now. Do you have any idea how lucrative the videogame business is? Our profits and royalties on *Dead Rite* alone were over seventy five million dollars, and we've created dozens of software packages for home computers and video games."

Torres grinned. "I just bought a copy of *Dead Rite* myself."

"Kiss ass," Fahey muttered.

"GameCo has only thirty six employees to share the profits ... oh, I'm sorry ... thirty five. I suppose some people will think that's good news. The profit-sharing checks will be even bigger this year. We have Gordon to thank for that." Ms. Reed smiled sweetly, as if she had just served them cookies.

Fahey leaned forward. "Are you saying Gordon Duffy had something to do with Mr. Shelton's murder?"

"Don't get me wrong, I like Gordon. Really, I do. But then, he *did* have a motive, didn't he?"

"How's that?" Torres asked.

"Why, that stock agreement."

14

The hands of the round government wall clock in Autopsy Suite B in the new central forensics facility stood at 6:25 p.m. The room and its equipment were state-of-the-art, and the walls and the floor gleamed with a military-like spit and polish. A powerful exhaust and air-conditioning system completely cleansed and recirculated the air in the room every ninety seconds; yet the fetor of death and decay was all but overpowering.

Leonard Hicks stood stiffly by the stainless steel examining table, his hands clasped behind his back, watching Dr. Charles Giese finish the autopsy on Case #98114. Samuel Shelton had been rendered to a number and a heap of butchered meat.

Dr. Giese seemed to enjoy his work. He hummed show tunes as he cut and snipped and sawed and probed away at the stinking mound of flesh and bone that lay upon the stainless steel examining table. His oddly handsome face was marred by an oversized proboscis, the tip of which was lined with tiny red broken capillaries. Hicks knew it was a drinker's nose, and wondered if Dr. Giese drank too much because he was a forensic pathologist, or if he was a forensic pathologist because he drank too much.

"How much longer, Charlie?" he asked, rocking back on his

heels. His back and legs were aching from the hours of standing.

"Not long." Dr. Giese sewed quickly, not bothering to use surgeons' stitches; simply tacking the flaps of skin together as if he were stitching up a Thanksgiving turkey. "No sense trying to be too tidy. Poor bastard's such a mess anyway. How about a cup of coffee? There's a bottle of Irish whiskey in the bottom file drawer. Help yourself, and pour me one while you're at it."

Hicks found the bottle of whiskey stashed between the hanging files. He poured a couple of ounces into two Styrofoam cups and topped them off with coffee.

Dr. Giese covered the corpse with a sheet and deposited his latex gloves in the biohazard container. While he was washing his hands, he said, "In medical school we mixed formaldehyde with our coffee. Really puts hair on your chest."

"I'll bet."

"Your Mr. Shelton was a very lucky man." Dr. Giese said, leading Hicks to his desk.

"You're getting weird, Charlie."

"Well, I found an early cancer of the pancreas. His tumor was still too small to cause him any problems, but in a month or so, it would have grown to the size of a grapefruit. Pancreatic cancers are almost always inoperable. If I were him, and I had a choice, I'd take a bullet in the head any day."

"I'm sure he'd be happy to hear that."

"The gunshot wound was the cause of death. The slug entered the skull at the frontal bone, 48 millimeters above the left eye socket, and exited the skull in the right quadrant of the occipital bone. The exact location of the exit hole is difficult to determine. The skull was shattered, and what was left of that area of the brain had turned to mush, so it was impossible to run a probe through the wound to determine the exact angle of the bullet's path."

"Any tattooing around the wound?"

"There were microscopic traces of gunpowder embedded in the skin on his face, but they weren't confined to the area of the wound. I'd say the deceased was six to eight feet from the gun when he was shot."

"Blood alcohol level?"

"Point zero five percent. Decomposition could account for some of that. I suspect he'd had two or three drinks that day, but not within the last couple of hours before death."

"Anything indicate he'd been drugged or had been taking drugs?"

"No, nothing."

"Then it's your opinion, Charlie, that Shelton was conscious with all his faculties intact when he was shot?"

"I'd say so."

"Any estimate of the time of death?"

"Body's too badly decomposed for me give you a time with any accuracy." Dr. Giese studied a paper that was on his desk. "But Linda Cole faxed me her estimate."

"What'd the bug lady have to say?"

"The maggots say that the lucky bastard died a week ago Saturday night or early Sunday morning."

———

Hicks left the county forensics facility a little after 7:00 p.m. and drove back to the central station. He found Fahey and Torres eating pizza in the homicide conference room.

"How about a slice?" Hicks said, sitting down with them. "If there's enough?"

"Take a couple," Torres said, "We can't eat it all."

Hicks picked a slice from the box and took a bite. "Anything helpful from L.A.?"

Torres smirked, "We've got this case all but wrapped."

"Bullshit," Hicks said.

"Not entirely," Fahey said.

Hicks wiped his hands on a napkin and leaned back in his chair. "Convince me."

Torres started, "For one thing, we found Shelton's Jag—"

"No shit?"

Torres grinned. "And you're never going to believe where we found it."

"In our fucking visitor's lot," Fahey said.

Hicks squinted at them. "Here? Slow down. Who found it? Traffic division?"

"We did," Torres said, beaming.

"We had a hunch it'd be here," Fahey said.

"You guys shitting me? I send you to L.A., and you end up finding Shelton's car in our lot?"

Fahey and Torres spent the next half hour filling Hicks in on what they'd found at Shelton's condo in Beverly Hills and about their interview with Virginia Reed.

"I still don't get it," Hicks said when they'd finished. "The garage man told you Shelton had to drive to San Bernardino because Duffy had had an accident. Then he gets himself murdered at Big Bear. What made you think his Jag would be in our lot?"

Fahey opened a file folder, took out a sheet of paper, and slid it over to him. "This is a photo copy of the top page of a note pad we found next to the phone in Shelton's bedroom. When we got back here around 5:00, we turned the original over to the crime lab. Took them only a couple of minutes to bring out the impression."

Hicks adjusted his spectacles and stared at the copy for a long moment. "Directions to our office?"

"Interesting, huh?" Torres said.

Fahey nodded. "And look at the last word."

"*Hicks*?"

"That's what it looks like to us, too," Torres said.

Hicks looked at the copy again. "I don't get it."

"Looks like Shelton was driving up here to see you," Fahey said.

"You can't be serious."

78

Torres said, "He drove up to see someone. Your name's on the note pad along with the directions. I mean, it's possible." He grinned. "Guess we'd better add you to the suspect list."

"Not funny, Torres," Fahey said.

Hicks' jaw was working. "Well, one thing's for sure. He never saw me."

"But he must've met someone here," Torres said. "He just wouldn't walk away from his Jag."

Hicks was still staring at the note. "We're sure Shelton wrote this?"

"We lifted some samples of his handwriting," Torres said. "Crime lab says the impressions on the pad are almost certainly his handwriting."

"That's why we checked the visitors' lot," Fahey said. "It was a long shot, but there it was: Shelton's green Jag, covered with a week's load of dust." She handed Hicks a plastic evidence bag containing a crumpled piece of notepad. "We found this on the Jag's front console—the original of the directions to our office."

"Jesus Christ!" Hicks sucked in a deep breath and let it out in a long sigh.

"Wait 'til the Sheriff and the media hear this one! The missing vehicle in a homicide investigation sits in our lot for over a week without being noticed" Fahey said. "But it's not really that fucked up. Why should anyone notice it? No one in the department uses that lot. It's for visitors."

"Okay. Let's say you're right, and he drove up here to see me. Why would he do that?"

Torres grinned. "Maybe he knew he was gonna be whacked and wanted to report it to you first."

"I'm in no mood for jokes," Hicks told him. "Did you check with Reception and Dispatch to see if there's any record of Shelton visiting or calling me or anyone else in this building the day or night he was murdered?"

Torres nodded. "They're still checking."

"We also interviewed a Virginia Reed while we were there," Fahey said.

"Who's she?"

"Shelton's executive assistant," Torres said.

Fahey said, "Torres tried the redial button on Shelton's phone to see the last number Shelton called the day of his murder. It was Reed. Turns out she was expecting us to call and granted us an interview."

Torres jumped in, "And the first thing she tells us when we arrive at her apartment was—and I quote—'If you ask me, Gordon Duffy deserves a kiss'."

"For what?"

"For bumping off Shelton," Fahey said.

"She said that?"

"She sure as hell intimated it," Fahey said.

"You believe her?"

"I don't know." She took a sip from a can. "I think she *thinks* Duffy murdered her boss, but that may be wishful thinking."

"You saying she has it in for Duffy?"

"No, just the opposite. Reed was giving off all kinds of vibes. For instance, she always referred to Duffy as Gordon."

"So?"

"Well, she never called Shelton by his first name. It was always Mr. Shelton."

Hicks smiled. "Okay. She likes Duffy."

"*Really* likes him. And then she laid the hammer on us. She claims Shelton murdered his first wife."

"Far out, huh?" Torres said.

"But that is what the fucking lady said," Fahey added.

"Think she's a nut case?"

"I gotta admit, I thought so at first. So did Torres. But I think she really believes the asshole murdered his wife."

Hicks turned back to Fahey. "What else did she tell you?"

"Duffy had a motive."

"Seems Duffy and Shelton had some kind of stock agreement," Torres said. "If either one of 'em dies—BINGO—winner takes all."

"GameCo's stock is worth a couple of billion," Fahey said.

15

Sergeant Ben Jackson, another member of Hicks' homicide team, stuck his head in the door. "Hey, you guys working late again? Glad I caught ya'. Got some info that could relate to the case you're working on."

Jackson was a huge black man, nearly forty, with thinning hair and a black brush of a mustache. He was a potbellied, six-foot-three giant who weighed in at 295 pounds. Before joining the Sheriff's Department in 1994, Jackson played middle linebacker for the Detroit Lions. Network color men dubbed him Gentle Ben because his smile was as big and broad as the rest of him, and he always helped opposing quarterbacks to their feet after slamming them onto the turf. Now, after more than ten years in homicide, he was the department's rookie coach. He'd mentored Fahey and Torres, and they had the greatest respect for his ability as an officer and a teacher.

Jackson took a chair across from Hicks, grinning at Torres as he did. "How ya' doin' Chihuahua?" Jackson had a nickname for everyone.

"Great. You?" Torres answered.

"Okay. But the knee's been acting up again." He patted the

offending joint that was the cause of his leaving the NFL. "Hey, Red, what's a nice girl like you doing hanging out with these bums?"

She returned his smile. "They're okay. Torres could use a good ass kicking."

Hicks asked, "How's that arson-homicide case coming along, Ben?"

"Just about a wrap," Jackson answered. "ATF booked a suspect a couple of hours ago."

"Why are the Feds working the case?" Torres asked.

Jackson grinned at him. "Ya' mean you don't know it all, Chihuahua? Bureau of Alcohol, Tobacco and Firearms investigates all government property arsons. The fire and homicides took place smack in the middle of a national forest."

"Isn't that the case where some pyro nailed a man and woman in a trailer and fried 'em?" Fahey asked.

Jackson nodded. "Real bad one. The victim was a woody named Harry Perz. They had a helluva time identifying the woman. She turned out to be one Shelley Ricco, a waitress up in Running Springs. The Forest Service put the fire out before it had a chance to spread, but Perz and Ricco were toast."

"Who's the perp?" Torres asked.

"The Feds think it's the Ricco woman's ex-boyfriend; a backhoe jockey by the name of Vince Esty. Ricco and Esty broke up a couple of weeks back. Guy was pissed—real pissed—and was seen stalking her off and on after the breakup. Esty caught up with her in a bar the night of the fire. They had a big fight, she drove off while he was taking a leak; Perz picked her up at another bar down the road. At least, that's where her car was found. The Feds think Esty followed her to Perz's place. The dumb ass has no alibi; he claims he called it a night after Ricco ran out on him. Says he was home in bed, sleeping at the time of the burn. The Feds didn't buy it."

"Sounds like you're not too sure Esty's the perp," Hicks said.

Jackson shrugged. "You might say that. But then, we're never really sure about such things, are we? And who am I to argue with the Feds? It's just," he shrugged again, "well, I don't know. Esty's dumber than shit. And dumb's one thing, crazy's another. Esty just don't seem *tha*t crazy to me. You really gotta be nuts to toast two people like that."

"Well, it's the Feds' problem, not ours," Hicks told him. "What've you got for us?"

"I knew Shelton," Jackson said. "Met him a few years back when I was investigating his wife's death. Ya' know she died at the same place he did at Big Bear?"

Hicks nodded.

"I was assigned to check it out, to see if it was a homicide. Happened the winter of '97. It wasn't an El Niño winter, but still and all, it was wet and cold. Storms came in weekly cycles—lots of floods in the valleys and blizzards in the mountains. Shelton said he and his wife decided to spend a romantic winter weekend together at the Big Bear cabin, so they drove up on a Friday morning. He claimed that after they arrived, he got an urgent call from his office; some problem only he could solve. He left the cabin just as the snow started, telling his wife he'd be back that evening, and drove back to L.A. By the time the meeting was over, the storm was so bad he decided to spend the night in the city. The next day, the roads on top of the mountain were closed—it was one helluva storm—and she was snowed in for two days."

Hicks said, "The cabin's not that primitive. It must have been warm and well stocked."

"Bet your ass it was," Jackson said. "There were at least two cases of scotch and vodka up there. The lady was a drunk, and there she was, snowed in ... telephone and power lines down, feeding wood to a fire, with all the booze in the world to warm her insides."

"So she drank herself to death?" Fahey said.

Jackson nodded.

"That's not a homicide," Hicks said.

Jackson disagreed. "Maybe, but I still think it was murder one;

a cold-blooded, premeditated homicide. I just couldn't get the D.A. or anyone else to buy my theory. There was no hard evidence."

"You should've talked to his secretary," Fahey said. "She would've backed you up."

"You mean, the Reed woman? I did. She confirmed Shelton's story. Said he did drive back to L.A. for a meeting."

"Doesn't matter if he did or didn't," Hicks said. "Like the D.A. said, it's not hard evidence."

Jackson said, "Then how about this: Shelton called the cabin's caretaker the day before he and his wife drove up. Had him stock the place with two cases of booze."

"Now, that's a lot of proof," Torres quipped.

"Jesus. Shut up!" Fahey said.

"I nosed around a little more and discovered Shelton had hired a private weather service in Palatine, Illinois a month before—one that specializes in providing charter airlines and private pilots with super accurate forecasts. He hired the service specifically to track Pacific storms. He knew there'd be a blizzard up there, that his wife would be snowed in, and he left her alone with all that booze."

"Proves he sure was an asshole," Fahey said.

"An asshole and a murderer," Jackson insisted.

"Aw, man," Torres said, "we know how you feel. But his old lady drank the shit all by her lonesome."

"You guys know Shelton divorced his wife back in '92?" Jackson said.

Hicks shook his head. "He had another wife?"

"No, the same damn one," Jackson said. "He remarried her the year before she died at Big Bear. My guess is, he hated giving her half of everything he had in the community property settlement, so the motherfucker remarried her to get it all back, planning all along to kill her. In my book, that's murder one."

Hicks nodded. "You could be right, but proving it is another thing."

"Shit, I know. It just pisses me off that he got away with it."

The phone rang. Torres picked it up. He listened for a minute, thanked the caller and hung up. "Dispatch," he said. "They recorded a call from Shelton's cell phone at 8:47, January ten. Caller asked for Lieutenant Hicks. He was told you weren't in. He hung up without identifying himself."

"Why would he call you, Len?" Jackson asked.

"We've been wondering the same thing," Hicks grinned at him. "Like to help us out on this one, Ben?"

"Bet your ass I would!"

———

They spent the next two hours going over Hicks' autopsy notes and the forensic reports on the evidence that had accumulated since Shelton's body had been discovered the day before.

"The crime lab guys found a spent slug while they were sifting the dirt in the grave," Torres told them. "They turned it over to the firearms and explosives lab. The slug was badly deformed. Lab thinks it could be a .38 or nine-millimeter."

"Can't they do better than that?" Hicks asked.

Torres' eyes moved down the F&E report. "There was enough of it left to determine it was a reload—"

"Shooter couldn't afford new bullets?" Jackson said.

Torres grinned. "The price of ammo's been going up."

Hicks put in, "A lot of gun collectors reload spent casings."

"Duffy?" Fahey said.

Torres continued. "The slug was fired from a revolver with six lands and six grooves. Probably Smith & Wesson or a Colt Trooper."

Hicks scratched his chin and said, "Duffy told me he had a Smith & Wesson .38 in his collection."

Torres got the bug. "Hey, every hour that goes by, our chances of solving this get worse ..."

Jackson winked at Hicks. "Right out of Homicide 101."

"... so let's go to L.A. tonight, get a warrant, and check out his weapons," Torres suggested.

Hicks shook his head. "No way. It can wait until morning, if we even go. I have a feeling we won't find the weapon in Duffy's collection. The slug was a reload."

"So? Collectors use reloads."

"But mainly for target practice."

"If the shooter used reloads, he was either very cheap or very smart," Jackson said.

"No, cheap and crazy," Torres shot back. "Reloads can misfire."

"Right," Jackson said patiently. "But if the shooter used reloads because he knew the manufacturer couldn't be traced— and reloads can't be—that'd make him very smart."

"Okay, you got a point," Torres argued. "But if we start pressuring Duffy, he's gonna start making mistakes."

Hicks and Jackson exchanged glances. "You really convinced that Duffy's the perp?" Hicks asked.

"Aren't we all?"

"I'm trying to keep an open mind," Hicks said.

"You should, too," Jackson told Torres.

Hicks tried to stifle a yawn. He was tired and wanted to move on. "What about the car door handle?" he asked.

Fahey shuffled through the papers in her file folder. "There were no usable prints on it. It's at the crime lab now; they claim it's from an older red Jeep Cherokee. There's blue paint from another vehicle embedded in the scratches on its chrome."

"Enough to type the vehicle?" Hicks asked.

Fahey shook her head. "Blue paint. That's all they could determine."

"Hey!" Torres exclaimed. "Wasn't there a blue SUV parked in the driveway of the GameCo cabin when we arrived at the scene?"

"Yeah, but it was black," Fahey said.

"You're color blind. It was blue. Dark blue."

Fahey turned to Hicks for help. "You saw it, boss. Blue or black?"

"Could've been either one. Black or blue, it was Duffy's SUV."

"Yes!" Torres raised his fist in triumph. "He's the perp!"

"Because he owns a blue or black SUV? Try that out on the D.A.," Jackson said.

Hicks yawned again and looked at his watch. "Look, guys, it's been a long day. We're all tired. We can't really accomplish any more tonight. Let's call it a day."

"Hell of an idea. What's on the agenda for tomorrow?" Fahey asked.

Hicks said, "I'm meeting Duffy at his attorney's office in Beverly Hills at 10:00 tomorrow morning. Torres, you ride with me, and while I'm meeting with Duffy, you go to the Duffy residence and check out his gun collection. If he has a .38 or nine millimeter, bring it in for ballistics testing."

"I'll need a warrant," Torres said.

"You'll have one."

"LAPD and the Beverly Hills cops will try to muscle in on the case," Jackson warned.

"Too damn bad," Hicks said. "Sooner or later, they're going to find out we're working their territory."

"What about Ben and me?" Fahey asked.

"There's plenty for you two to do here. Wait for Torres' report, and query all our stations and the DMV. See if anyone has an accident report involving a Cherokee the night of the murder."

"You know, I've been thinking," Jackson said. "Maybe Red and I should check out the Big Bear scene. I could use the mobile crime lab. I got something that needs checking out along the way."

"Like?" Hicks asked.

Jackson shrugged. "Little early to say. May not be important. Then again, you never know."

"Okay," Hicks said. "Have the crime lab tag along. I'll get you a warrant, too, so you can tear that GameCo cabin apart."

———

Gordon Duffy was not having a good night. He'd just dozed off when the phone rang. He fumbled for it, only to find Sharon Grant's angry voice on the other end of the line.

"Duffy, I can't hack it. You gotta come over. There are *things* in my fucking bedroom."

"Whatever you're seeing can't hurt you."

"Listen, goddamn it! Get your ass over here! If you're not here in five minutes, I'm having a fucking drink!" She hung up the phone and he climbed out of bed.

Jen felt him leave her side. Blinking the sleep from her eyes, she peered at the clock radio, which read 12:16 a.m. She let out a low moan as he padded to his walk-in closet. "Why can't your sotty friends call at a decent hour?" she complained.

"Sorry. This is when most people need help."

"Not most people, luv. Just your bloody drunks. When are you going to stop playing savior to the world's alcoholics?"

"I'm an alcoholic," he reminded her, pulling on a pair of pants.

"You *were* an alcoholic," she corrected.

"Once a lush always a lush."

"Rubbish! You haven't had a drink in years. It's time you let someone else do the dirty work." She watched him come out of the closet. "Is that all you're going to wear, luv? Put on a sweater or something."

He went back into the closet and pulled on a sweatshirt. "Helping other drunks helps keep me sober."

"You might try thinking of me sometime."

He slipped into a pair of scruffy topsiders, went to the bed, and kissed her on the forehead. "I'm sorry. I don't like to wake you like this."

"I'm sorry, too. I know you have to do it. Who's the poor bugger this time?"

"New member," he lied. "Lives in Brentwood. I should be home in a couple of hours. Go back to sleep."

16

The yellow crime scene tape that hung around the burnt-out remains of Harry Perz's trailer and Cherokee flapped gently in the morning breeze when Jackson's unmarked black Ford Crown Victoria drove up the gravel drive at 8:30 the next morning. It was followed by a mobile crime lab van; a mud-splattered Dodge pickup was at the end of the drive.

"Looks like we've got ourselves some company," Jackson said, pulling up beside the remains of the Cherokee.

Fahey said. "Think it's the ATF?"

"Naw," Jackson said as he and Fahey climbed out of the car. "Feds wouldn't be seen dead in that old heap."

"The pyro?"

He shook his head. "I kinda doubt it."

The driver of the crime lab van rolled down his window and shouted, "Hey, Ben. Why the fuck you stopping here?"

Jackson called back. "I wanna check something."

Fahey followed Jackson past what was left of the trailer. "Bitch of a way to go."

"No kidding. The last thing I wanna end up as is toast," he said.

"Oh, I don't know. Think I'll be cremated."

"Thought the Church didn't allow cremation."

"I don't want a bunch of fucking drunk Micks leering into my casket at a wake."

"You'll be dead, so who cares?"

They'd reached the rusting remains of the Cherokee. He pointed to the left rear door—it was missing a handle. He pulled a plastic evidence bag from his coat pocket and fitted it into the door. "I'll be damned, Red. A perfect match. I don't know how the damn thing got in Shelton's pocket, but it came from this heap."

"We better have the lab guys confirm it."

As they started for the crime lab van, a shout came from the woods at the far end of the clearing. "Roooooodeeeeeee!"

It stopped them in their tracks. Jackson reached for his gun and said, "Must be the guy from the pickup."

A young man came out of the woods carrying a metal pie pan. He shouted again, "Rooooooodeeeeeeee!"

"Hey!" Jackson yelled at him.

The man stalked toward them. "Hey, yourself. You're trespassing. Now, get off this property, or I'll call the sheriff!"

Jackson opened his badge case and held it up. "We're with the Sheriff's Department, and you're the one who's trespassing. This is an official crime scene."

"Aw shit, not again." The pie pan he was carrying was heaped with dog food. "I'm looking for my dog, a German shepherd. Haven't seen him since the fire."

Jackson took out his notebook. "Name?"

"Rudy."

"Not the dog, sir. You—are you a relative of the deceased?"

"Oh, yeah. I'm Jerry Perz. His brother."

Fahey asked, "You live with him?"

He shook his head. "I've got an apartment down in Ontario."

"What was your dog doing here the night of the fire?" she asked.

"I'm a United flight attendant. My roommates don't like dogs, so Rudy was staying with Harry until I could find a place of my own. I can't understand what happened to him. I know he was here when I left the night of the fire."

"You were here the night of the fire?" Jackson asked.

"I always come up to play with Rudy on weekends if I'm not on a trip. That Saturday was kinda special ... Rudy's first birthday."

Jackson said, "I was here the morning after the place was torched. Forensics didn't find any animal bones when they sifted the ashes."

"Well, he was here." Perz turned and pointed toward the tool shed. "I chained him up over there before I left. The fire musta spooked him and he musta broke loose."

"Fires do scare the shit out of animals," Jackson agreed.

Fahey went to the shed and examined the dog's chain and collar. "Your brother ever take Rudy off his chain?"

"No way. Harry didn't like Rudy; he only let me keep him here because I told him he was a good watchdog. But he really wasn't. He hardly ever barked."

Fahey said, "Maybe Harry just turned him loose. The chain's not broken and it's still fastened to the collar. It's been unbuckled. Ever know a dog that could unbuckle his own fucking collar?"

"Harry'd never let him go. He knew I'd kill him if he did."

———

Fahey helped Jerry Perz comb the perimeter of the clearing for any signs of his missing German shepherd. Jackson's knee was killing him, so he decided to sit in his car and give it a few minutes rest. To pass the time, he ran the pickup's plates and found that Jerry's pickup was registered to Harry, the deceased. His curiosity aroused, Jackson ran the plates of the Cherokee and found it was registered to Jerry. For some reason, the Perz brothers had swapped vehicles. Jackson climbed out of his car and limped over to Perz. "Hey, I got another question for you, Jerry. When did you and your brother swap vehicles?"

"It wasn't a swap. I just borrowed Harry's pickup, that's all."

"When?"

"Uh, about a week ago, I guess."

"You guess? Come on, you can do better than that. You were here the night of the fire, and that's your Cherokee burnt to a crisp over there. What are we supposed to think?"

Perz blinked as if he'd been slapped. "No way! Harry was my brother. My *twin* brother. I didn't do this! I'd never hurt him."

"Like Cain couldn't hurt Abel," Jackson said.

"Hey, fuck you! I'm not saying another damn word, not unless you help me find Rudy."

"Ten to one he did it," Fahey quipped.

Jackson winked at her. "I'd better cuff him."

"Oh, I don't think there's any need for that, Ben," she said, playing the good cop. "Let's take him back to your car and give him time to think about it."

They put Perz in the back of the Crown Victoria and locked the doors. The rear seat was a reinforced compartment designed for transporting prisoners, separated from the front and rear cargo by inch-thick, shatterproof Plexiglas shields. The sun was climbing higher, so Jackson and Fahey sat up front with their side doors open to let in what little breeze there was. The only ventilation for the rear seat area was a small circle of holes drilled through the Plexiglas shield. Jackson poured her a cup of muddy coffee from his thermos. She took a sip and grimaced.

"Jesus, Ben, this is really strong shit."

"Mmm, yeah. Just the way I like it."

She took a county road map from the glove compartment and began to fan herself. "Gonna be a hot one."

"Sure is." He looked at Perz in the rear view mirror. He still wasn't sweating enough. "Tell me, Red. How you like working with Len?"

"He's great. A really great boss. I truly love the man. Only ..."

"Only what?"

"Now, don't get me wrong, but sometimes I feel like I'm his daughter or something."

He laughed. "Shit, Red, what's so bad about that? I mean, he's got three of 'em. Oldest one's about your age."

"Yeah, I know. But it gets kind of embarrassing. He doesn't treat me the same as Torres."

"Like?"

"He's always opening doors for me ... and he makes me get on elevators first ... you know, shit like that ..."

This time Jackson laughed so hard it shook the whole car. "Red, he's from a different time. He was raised to think that women need protection. In other words, he's a goddamn old-fashioned gentleman. In the truest sense of the word: a gentle man. I tell you one thing, he sure as hell knows what a good cop you are."

"I'm dying back here!" Perz complained through the holes. "Open the windows!"

"You and your fucking coffee, Ben," she said, ignoring them both. "Now I gotta pee."

"There's an outhouse."

"I don't think I can handle some backcountry shithouse."

"Then there's always the woods."

Fahey groaned. "Goddammit. Be right back."

She climbed out of the car and headed for the outhouse. Ben watched the door close behind her, and a few seconds later, it flew open, Fahey screaming, "Oh, shit! That's fucking disgusting!"

Jackson grinned as she ran back to the car. "Can't be that bad, Red."

"Says you. I found the fucking dog!"

"You found Rudy?" Perz asked, pressed against the Plexiglas.

She was in no mood to be kind. "Yeah. Somebody stuffed him down the middle shit hole."

17

A little past 10:00 that morning, Hicks met with Gordon Duffy and Matthew Baldwin in the cherry-paneled main conference room at the Beverly Hills offices of Crawford, Raskin, Lutz, and Baldwin. Baldwin sat at the end of the conference table nearest the door. A silver tray with a coffee carafe and three bone china cups and saucers sat in front of him. Hicks took the chair to Baldwin's left, while Duffy sat to his right. A court reporter was poised at her Stenotype machine in the far corner, ready to take down every word.

Hicks had thought the meeting would be more or less an informal interview and couldn't help wondering why Baldwin acted like his client was about to be deposed. Placing his battered briefcase next to his chair, he unfastened its clasp and took out his notebook and a microcassette recorder. "Any objection to my recording the meeting?" he asked Baldwin, placing the recorder on the conference room table.

"No, but it's not necessary," Baldwin said, lining up half a dozen pencils next to his yellow legal pad. "We'll fax you a transcript."

Hicks pressed the record button anyway. The court reporter's fingers were already flying across the keys of her machine.

"There are two points I'm willing to concede from the beginning," Baldwin began, reaching for the carafe on his desk. "Coffee?" he asked.

"I could use a cup," Duffy said.

"Lieutenant?" Baldwin asked, holding up the carafe.

Hicks stifled a yawn and said, "Thanks, I could use one, too." He realized he wasn't the only one who had lost sleep the night before. Duffy appeared weary and haggard, and Baldwin's light blue eyes were red-rimmed.

"Cream and sugar?" the lawyer asked.

"Black," Duffy said.

"Same here," Hicks said.

Baldwin handed them their cups. Then he put two lumps of sugar in his own cup and took a sip. "First of all," he started, "we know the murder occurred sometime between Saturday night, January ten, and Sunday morning, January eleven."

"Agreed," Hicks said.

Baldwin went on, "I'm willing to concede my client has no alibi for that time period. Mr. Duffy was alone at the GameCo cabin the entire weekend, working the bugs out of a new game he's designing. He retired early Saturday night, sometime around 10:00, and slept until about 8:00 Sunday morning. After a light breakfast, he continued working on the game without a break until about 4:00 that afternoon. Then he drove back to his home in Bel Air. During the entire time he was at Big Bear, he neither saw nor spoke to anyone. So, we have no witnesses to confirm his whereabouts the weekend of the murder."

Hicks put down his cup and saucer. "So, your first point is, your client has no alibi. What's the second point you'll concede?"

"When you were questioning my client the day Mr. Shelton's body was discovered, did he inform you that he has a gun collection?"

"Yes."

"Did he reveal that information to you before you explained his legal rights?"

"I never informed him of his rights."

"Then you're aware that his statement is not admissible?"

"Yes, I know the law, counselor. Your client wasn't a suspect at the time I interviewed him. He was merely a witness. There's no requirement that witnesses have to be advised of their rights."

"But you do concede that any statements Mr. Duffy made about his weapons collection cannot be entered into evidence if this case goes to trial?"

"That's arguable."

"But that's a pretty thin legal line to walk. It's very difficult to prove exactly when the investigatory stage passes into the accusatory stage. I'm sure a judge would rule that you did consider my client a suspect when he made that statement. But I'm not here to quibble points of law with you."

"So, what's your point?"

"Mr. Duffy is willing to accede to your demand."

"I don't recall demanding anything of him."

"You did inform my client that you'd like to see his gun collection?"

"Yes."

"I want to prove to you that we intend to cooperate with you in this investigation," Baldwin said. "When this meeting is over, you may accompany Mr. Duffy and myself to his residence where you may examine his collection."

"That won't be necessary," Hicks said with a small smile. "One of my detectives is on his way to Mr. Duffy's residence as we speak."

Baldwin's eyes narrowed. "I hope he has a warrant."

"He does. Now, if that's all you're willing to concede, can we proceed with the interview?"

———

Torres drove up to the Duffy residence on Bellflower, a cul-de-sac backing up to the Bel Air Country Club, at 10:32 a.m. He was impressed by the white contemporary home—something right out of *Architectural Digest*—it was the kind crib he'd buy when he won the lottery. He rang the bell, identified himself to the maid, and asked to see Mrs. Duffy. The frightened maid took one look at his detective's shield and hurried up the stairs to the second floor, leaving him cooling his heels at the door. He was still standing there five minutes later when Jen Duffy came down the staircase wearing a red silk Hana Mori robe over a wispy white nightgown. She had no makeup on and her long, ash brown hair seemed to have been hastily brushed. Torres struggled not to stare at the curves under her robe.

"Yes?" she said.

"Sorry, ma'am. I'm Detective—"

"My maid told me who you are. What do you want?"

"I have a search warrant." He took the document from his inside coat pocket. "This is a court order authorizing me to search your house for a .38 caliber or nine-millimeter handgun."

She held out her hand to him. "May I see it?"

Torres handed it to her, and after she lowered her eyes to read it, he stared admiringly at her, thinking that she was *muy malo*, but knowing that she wouldn't be acting so cool if she knew what a great lover he was.

"You won't have to search the house," she said in a slightly warmer tone. "If we have what you're looking for, it'll be in my husband's gun collection. Come. I'll show it to you. It's in his study."

Torres followed her up the spiral staircase to the second floor. Her hips undulated beneath the slippery silk as she climbed the steps ahead of him. He couldn't help staring at the motion with fascination, his antennae picking up her vibes. This is one sexy lady, he told himself.

She led him into her husband's study and showed him the gun cabinet built into the far wall. "I don't know a thing about guns. Is what you're looking for in there?"

Torres peered through the cabinet's glass doors. His eyes were quick to spot the .38. There's a .38 Smith & Wesson in there, all right. Between the Colt .45 and the Beretta." He took a pair of latex gloves from his pocket and pulled them on.

"My husband always keeps it locked."

"Where's the key?"

"In his desk. But it's always locked, too."

He studied the cabinet's lock for a moment. "Mind if I try opening it? It's not much of a lock."

"You have the warrant."

He reached down and took the switchblade from his boot, and he slipped the long, thin blade between the cabinet doors, twisting it slightly. The lock snapped open.

"What good are locks?"

"I try to make everything seem easy, ma'am." He took the .38 out of the cabinet and slipped it into a plastic evidence bag. "Where does he keep his loads?"

"Loads?"

"Ammo. Bullets?"

"In the cabinet drawers. They're always locked, too."

Torres squatted down on his haunches and inserted the blade of his knife into the opening above the top drawer and snapped the lock open. It contained boxes of rifle and shotgun shells, but no .38 ammo. He closed the drawer, and forced the bottom drawer lock. He found what he was looking for and held up a box of .38 reloads for her to see. "Mind if I take this, too? We need some ammo to test the gun."

"I suppose the court order entitles you to take anything you want."

Torres stood up to his full height. He was only slightly taller than she, but the way she was looking at him made him feel six feet tall. "Not without your permission, ma'am. The warrant only covers the gun and ammo."

She moved closer to him. "I hate guns. Take what you want.

There's more in the basement—all his equipment and a practice range."

18

While the mobile crime lab technicians, Don Merkle and his assistant, Penny Howard, extracted Rudy's carcass from the outhouse pit and washed the shit and maggots off with a hose, Jerry Perz was spilling his guts to Jackson and Fahey.

"The day of the fire, Harry and I had dinner at this little dive up by Rolling Springs. Harry was looking to get lucky, so he drove the pickup, and I drove the Cherokee. We'd had a few beers too many and about 9:00 this girl came into the bar—"

"Shelley Ricco?" Fahey asked.

"Yeah, but I didn't know her name until I read it in the papers. Anyway, Harry knew her, and she was really upset. She'd had a fight with her man and was afraid to go home. Like I said, he was just looking to get lucky."

Jackson said, "Guess it wasn't his night."

"I stayed behind to pay the check then started back to Harry's place to say goodbye to Rudy. On the way down the mountain, I ran into a fog bank. Probably a low cloud. It was real thick. The glare of my own headlights blinded me. Then I saw a pair of headlights coming at me. I'd crossed the center line. I tried to turn back to my side of the road, but sideswiped the other car."

"Did you stop or keep going?"

"We both stopped. On opposite shoulders. I was scared shitless."

"Did you actually see the other vehicle?"

"Yeah. It was dark and foggy, but it was some kind of SUV. A big one. Like a Suburban or Expedition."

"What color?" Fahey asked.

"Can't say. Like I said, it was dark and foggy and I'd had a few beers."

"Did you report the accident?" Jackson asked.

"Didn't have to," Perz said.

"Oh?" Fahey said.

"The other driver was a deputy sheriff."

"A deputy? You sure?" Jackson asked.

"Yeah. That's why I switched my Cherokee for Rudy's pickup."

Jackson and Fahey exchanged glances.

"I'm not following you," Fahey said.

"Look. I'm a flight attendant. I had a 6:50 a.m. trip to Chicago. I was a little drunk. We're not supposed to drink twenty-four hours before a flight. Most people—even Captains—ignore the rule once in a while. But I had to go and have an accident with a fucking deputy sheriff. Guess it was *my* lucky night—the deputy was in a hurry, and he let me off with a warning when I told him I lived down the road at Harry's place. Now I was really scared shitless. I couldn't drive my heap down to Ontario. I thought the deputy might radio his buddies down the mountain to be on the lookout for the Cherokee, and I couldn't stay with Harry; he had the Ricco chick at his place. So I drove down there to ask if I could borrow his pickup. He didn't give a shit. All he wanted to do was to get rid of me so he could get back to banging Shelley."

"Did the deputy show you his badge or any ID?" Fahey asked.

Perz shook his head.

"Then how can you be sure he was a deputy?" she asked.

"Well, that's what the other guy said."

"There was someone with him?" Jackson asked.

"Yeah, it was the other guy who told me the deputy was a deputy."

"But you saw his ID?" Fahey said.

"Like I said, I was a little drunk. You don't question cops when you've been in an accident and you're a little drunk."

"You remember what the deputy looked like?" Jackson asked.

"Yeah, he was a big guy."

"Would you recognize him if you saw him again?"

"Maybe."

"How about the other guy? Was he a deputy, too?"

"I don't know. He was older. I just saw him for a minute by the headlights of a semi that roared past us. He'd come up to the deputy when he was talking to me, and I don't know why, but that really pissed off the deputy. He ordered him to go back to his car, calling him Mr. Something or other. Can't remember the name."

"Remember anything else about the deputy?"

"No, not really. But I got his name." Perz pulled out his billfold. "Got it right here. He wrote my name in his notebook and gave me this." He took a folded piece of notepaper and handed it to Jackson. "Said he'd call me in the morning."

Jackson's eyes widened as he stared at the name. "Oh, shit!" He handed the paper to Fahey.

She blinked at the name scribbled on it. "Deputy Hicks? Fuck."

Jackson nodded. "Let's take a walk, Red."

They climbed out of the car.

"Can I get out?" Perz asked. "It's hotter than hell."

"I'll open the door for you," Jackson said, unlocking the back door. "But you stay put until we say you can go."

Jackson walked Fahey out of earshot, before he asked, "Think Hicks is involved with this?"

"No fucking way."

"It's the second time his name's come up."

Fahey turned on Jackson, her Irish up. "Honest to God, Ben,

you actually think he's involved?"

"No, but we can't ignore it. You know that."

"You'd turn on him?"

"Internal Investigations has to know. That's the rules."

"Fuck you, Ben. I'm not ratting on Hicks." She started stomping back toward the car.

Jackson caught her by the arm. "Let's make a deal, Red. I'll call the office and have them fax us Hicks' file photo. If Perz can't ID him, I'll call Hicks and let him decide if we report it or not."

"Deal," Fahey said with a grin.

After Jackson called the office, he limped to the tool shed, where Don Merkle and his assistant, Penny Howard, were still cleaning the dog's carcass. "How's it coming?" he asked.

Merkle looked up and said, "We got most of the shit off the mutt, but the fucker's still a mess."

"So I smell," Jackson said.

His assistant said, "The dog's been shot."

"You kidding?" Jackson got down on his haunches to take a closer look.

"Someone stuck a gun in its mouth and blew half its jaw off," Merkle said.

"What the hell?" Jackson stood up. "Shit. Have an autopsy performed on it."

"Who the fuck does autopsies on dogs?" Merkle asked.

"Call Dispatch and have somebody from animal control pick up the carcass and take it to a vet. If there's a bullet in that mutt, I want it."

Jackson limped back to the car.

"The fax of Hicks' file photo is coming in," Fahey told him.

They waited for the fax to be printed out, then showed it to Perz.

"Is this the deputy who told you his name was Hicks?" Jackson asked.

Perz stared at the fax for a long moment. "It's kinda fuzzy. And like I said—"

"You were a little drunk," Fahey said.

"Yeah. And it was dark. But I'm sure it's not him. The guy I talked to wasn't that old or that bald."

19

Hicks was still interviewing Duffy in Matthew Baldwin's office when his cell phone rang, and he saw it was Ben Jackson.

"Sorry," Hicks apologized to Baldwin. "One of my detectives needs to talk to me. Mind if I step away?"

"No, but would you mind using a land line, Lieutenant? Some cell phones interfere with interoffice security. There's an empty office right down the hall. I'll take you to it." He stood up and told Duffy and the court reporter to take a break, then he escorted Hicks to a vacant office. "Just dial eight for an outside line."

"Thanks," Hicks said. He went behind the desk and picked up the receiver. "Mind closing the door when you leave?"

Baldwin smiled at Hicks. "You don't remember me, do you?"

"You headed the Ray Keller defense team. I was a prosecution witness."

"A very hostile one."

"Close the door," Hicks said, ungraciously.

After Baldwin was gone, he picked up the phone and dialed Jackson's cell phone number. It took Jackson the better part of ten minutes to fill in Hicks on what he and Fahey had found at the Harry Perz crime scene that morning. When he finished his monologue, Jackson asked, "Kinda weird, isn't it?"

"Damn weird," Hicks agreed.

"So, what do we do now?"

Hicks had to think for a moment. "Well, I suppose the first thing you'd better do is inform Internal Investigations that my name came up again."

"I don't see why," Jackson said. "Perz has pretty much let you off the hook."

"Maybe. But the guy who sideswiped Perz that night claimed he was Deputy Hicks. I know the guy wasn't me, and now you know he wasn't me, but that's not good enough. It's got to be investigated."

"I agree. But we can handle it. It's not an internal affair."

"It is if the guy who claimed he was me actually *was* a deputy."

"You think the perp could be one of us?"

"Anything's possible."

"But it's just as likely the guy was bullshitting Perz."

After thinking it over for a moment, Hicks said. "Why don't we see if Perz can ID Duffy? That's enough proof to link Duffy to Shelton."

"Want me to hold him as a material witness?"

"Not if he's willing to cooperate."

"He claims he has a trip tonight, the red eye from L.A. to Chicago. It's a turn-around run—gets him back into LAX about 10:00 tomorrow. If I ask him to cancel the trip, he can always say no."

"He won't have to cancel. Torres took a video of Duffy at the crime scene. Have Perz stop by the office on his way back to Ontario and take a look at it. If he IDs Duffy we could wrap this up today. If not, Duffy's off the hook."

"And we have no suspect."

Hicks hung up and returned to the conference room.

———

Before they continued the interview, Baldwin reminded Duffy once again of his rights. "You can refuse to answer any question Deputy Hicks asks. If I think a question is leading, or that your reply could be prejudicial, I'll advise you not to answer. But refusing to answer does not imply guilt in any way."

"I understand," Duffy said. "I've nothing to hide."

Hicks opened his notebook and stared thoughtfully at it for a long moment, then looked up at Duffy, trying to pick up where he had left off. "You say you didn't see anyone the entire weekend?"

"That's right."

"And you didn't speak to anyone? Not even on the telephone?"

"I had a couple of phone conversations Saturday evening and one Sunday morning."

"With whom?"

"Brandon Cash called me sometime between 5:00 and 6:00."

"Who's Cash?"

"A young man who works for me."

"At GameCo?"

"No, at my home. Brandon's a law student. He does odd jobs for me and my wife."

"Like what?"

"Handyman sort of things. Pays for his room and board."

"He lives in your home?"

"Yes. In an apartment above our coach house."

"Why did he call?"

"There was some problem. I can't remember what. Something to do with the plumbing."

"Who else called?"

"My wife."

"What time?"

"Sometime between 9:00 and 10:00 Saturday night, and again the next morning."

"What were the conversations about?"

"The Saturday call was about a movie she'd seen in Westwood

that evening. It was an English film. One of those Gothic romances. Can't remember the name. I'm not into them."

"The Sunday morning call?"

"She wanted to know when I would be home."

"Did you talk to anyone else on the telephone that weekend?"

"No. Not that I can recall."

"You didn't call Samuel Shelton between 5:45 and 7:15 that evening?"

"No."

Hicks changed his tack, trying to catch Duffy off guard. "Did you and Shelton have some sort of stock agreement?"

Duffy looked to Baldwin for help.

"I really don't want to go into the stock agreement now," Baldwin told Hicks. "The agreement was prepared by one of the firm's senior partners. I just learned about it yesterday afternoon, so I don't know enough to advise my client on the subject. If you wish, I can turn a copy of the document over to you once I've had time to digest it."

Hicks nodded his agreement. "Do you own a dark blue or black SUV?"

"Yes, a black Lincoln Navigator."

"Own any other vehicles?"

"A Mercedes."

"What color?"

"Sort of bronze."

"Which vehicle did you drive up to Big Bear that weekend?"

"The Mercedes. The Navigator's my wife's car."

"But you do drive it, too."

"Yes."

"Has the SUV been in any kind of accident recently?"

"No."

Hicks thumbed back a few pages in his notebook, then looked at Duffy over the top of his glasses. "Mr. Duffy, are you a member of Alcoholics Anonymous?"

"You don't have to answer that," Baldwin advised.

Duffy ignored him. "Yes. I've never made a secret of it."

"When we talked last Saturday, you said Sharon Grant is an alcoholic."

Baldwin interrupted, "I don't see what Ms. Grant's drinking history has to do with anything."

"We've been told your client and Samuel Shelton argued the week before the murder," Hicks explained. "Apparently, it was over Sharon Grant." He turned back to Duffy. "Is that correct?"

"Don't answer that," Baldwin warned.

Duffy looked confused.

"Was it a love triangle? Were you both involved with Sharon Grant?" Hicks pressed, trying to anger Duffy into answering.

"No way," Duffy growled.

"What was the argument about?" Hicks asked.

"You don't have to answer that," Baldwin advised again.

"I know, but I think I should," Duffy shot back. "Sharon is an alcoholic. I sponsored her in AA several months ago. It wasn't working out. She couldn't stop drinking as long as she was living with Sam."

"Was Shelton an alcoholic?" Hicks asked.

"No. He drank. A lot. But he could walk away from it. Sharon couldn't. I'm not sure if she loved him, but she loved to party. So did he. I warned him that she had a drinking problem. He seemed to think it was a joke."

"So you moved her out?"

"Yes."

"Against her will?"

"She wanted to leave him; she couldn't walk out without help."

"When did you do it?"

"A couple of weeks ago."

"A week or so before Shelton was murdered?"

"Yes."

"And that's why you and he argued?"

"He claimed I had no right to interfere with his personal life. I couldn't convince him that I wasn't interfering. I was trying to save her life!"

"Were you able to keep him away from her?"

Duffy nodded. "She's been drying out at the home of a friend, Geoffrey Seaman. He's in Europe, directing a film. Before he left, he gave me permission to use his home. Sam never found out where we'd taken her."

"We?"

"Brandon Cash and me. I'm also his AA sponsor."

Hicks scribbled a few lines in his notebook. "We've been trying to interview Sharon Grant. How can I reach her?"

Duffy gave Hicks the address and phone number of Geoff Seaman's house in Bel Air. After
jotting them down in his notebook, he studied a page for a few moments, then looked up at Duffy.

"Did you kill Samuel Shelton?"

"Now wait a minute!" Baldwin bellowed.

"It's okay," Duffy cut him off. "No. I had nothing to do with Sam's death."

"Would you be willing to take a lie detector test?" Hicks shot back.

Baldwin jumped to his feet and ended the interview. "You're way out of line, Lieutenant! You know lie detector tests aren't admissible. No client of mine will take a test that can't possibly prove or disprove his innocence."

———

It was a little past noon when Hicks came out the revolving doors of Baldwin's building on West Beverly Boulevard. He spotted his SUV parked in a red zone, opened the door on the passenger's side, and climbed in next to Torres. "Been waiting long?"

"Not more than an hour," Torres grunted. He held up a plastic evidence bag. "Look what I've got. Thirty-eight Smith & Wesson. I phoned the serial number into FEU. They're checking to see if Duffy registered it."

"Good. We've had a very productive morning. Hungry? How about getting a bite to eat? Somewhere close. We only got an hour or so before we interview Sharon Grant."

"Sharon Grant?" Torres yelled, pulling into traffic. "You shitting me?!"

"Duffy gave me her number. I called her from the lobby and set up a 1:00 interview. She's staying in Bel Air."

Torres drove to the only restaurant he knew that was nearby——the Hamburger Hamlet on South Beverly where he and Fahey ate lunch nearly every day.

After the waitress brought their orders, Torres took a huge bite from his guacamole burger. "So, Duffy's old lady is one hot piece of ass."

"Oh? I thought you were investigating him, not her."

"I'm very intuitive when it comes to chicks. And man, was she coming on to me! I could feel the vibes in my pants!"

Hicks nodded at a blue-haired woman sitting at a nearby table. "If that little old lady over there smiled at you, you'd think she was hot for you."

"Who's to say she's not?"

Hicks took a bite from the Hotsburger Torres had recommended, and it brought beads of sweat to his forehead. "Jesus! What's in this thing?"

Torres laughed, "Really good shit, huh?"

Hicks took a sip of ice water to cool the heat of the jalapeño pepper cheese, then coughed before asking, "Come up with anything else?"

"Couple of boxes of .38 reloads."

Hicks took another sip of water.

Torres sucked his malt through the straw. "The fine wife told me that Duffy reloads all his used shell casings. She took me to his layout in the basement. He's got a regular gun shop down there and his own fucking target range."

"She volunteered to show it to you?"

"Like I said, she was really turning it on. I could've had her if I wasn't on official business. She even let me have these." Torres reached into his pocket and pulled out a baggie of deformed bullets and handed it to Hicks.

He studied the bag's contents for a moment before he said, "Spent .38 slugs?"

"Yeah. There's a whole can of slugs on his workbench. She said to help myself, but I only took the .38s."

"I'm beginning to think maybe you did fuck her, Torres," Hicks said.

Torres grinned, showing his perfect teeth. "I also talked her out of these." He handed Hicks an envelope that contained two snapshots. One was a recent photo of Duffy riding in a golf cart; the other was a snapshot of Sharon Grant with a man taken at a party.

"Shelton?" Hicks asked.

"You've got it. Taken at GameCo's Christmas party last month." Torres pulled out a toothpick and started to chew. "The asshole looks a little different than when we dug him up."

Hicks looked at his watch. "We'd better get going. We don't want to miss our appointment with Sharon."

Torres beamed. "Sharon? We're on a first-name basis with her fine ass, too? What a day!"

Hicks picked up the check and the envelope of photos. "Let's fax these to Ben and Fahey.   They've got a witness who may be able to ID them."

———

Baldwin left Duffy in the cherry-paneled conference room while he showed the court reporter to an office where she could download and print out the transcript of the meeting with Hicks. It would be forty-three pages long.

Before he returned to his client, Baldwin checked with his secretary to see if he had any messages, briefly discussed another case he was handling with one of the firm's paralegals, and went into the office Hicks had used to call Ben Jackson. He sat down at the desk, took a legal pad from the middle drawer, picked up the telephone receiver, and entered his personal pin number to access the firm's computer. He listened to the conversation the computer had recorded, occasionally jotting a note on the yellow pad.

When Baldwin finally returned to the conference room, he apologized to Duffy. "Sorry to keep you waiting. Had some loose ends to tie up."

"That's okay," Duffy said. "How do you think the meeting went?"

The leather in Baldwin's chair creaked as he leaned forward on his elbows. "How do you think it went?"

"I don't know. Hicks doesn't seem like a bad guy."

"Don't kid yourself. He's out to get you."

Duffy appeared as if it had never occurred to him that someone might be out to get him. "I don't know why—"

"For God's sake, get real! All the evidence points to you."

"It's all circumstantial, isn't it?"

"Yes, but many a man's been hung by circumstantial evidence. Look at it from Hicks's point of view: Shelton's body was found on your property, you were there at the time he was murdered, you have no alibi, you had a motive, and you own a gun that matches the murder weapon."

"But I'm not guilty!"

"Can you prove it?"

"I could if I had to."

"How?"

Duffy didn't answer.

Baldwin pounded his desk with his fist. "Are you fucking nuts? Do want to go to the gas chamber or spend the rest of your life in prison? How can I defend you if you tie my hands behind my back? If you want me to help you, you've got to tell me everything."

Duffy contemplated the gas chamber for a moment before he asked, "Will it be just between the two of us?"

"Of course. Anything you tell me is protected and privileged."

20

Brandon Cash and Sharon Grant were reclining on chaises by the pool at Geoffrey Seaman's house in Bel Air. It turned out to be one of those warm sunny California days that can happen in January. They had been sitting there since midmorning, soaking up the sun between El Niño showers, and catching up on their homework. For the first time in weeks, Sharon was reading a script. Cash was working his way through a stack of law books, boning up for his winter final exams, which were scheduled to begin the following week.

She dropped the script in her lap. "God, I could sure use a beer."

"I know the feeling."

"You've been dry for over a year," she said, removing her sunglasses. "How long does it take to get over the urge to drink?"

"You never get over it."

She rolled her eyes. "That's such fucking good news!"

Brandon watched her get up from the chaise. She was wearing a plum-colored maillot suit that fit like it was sprayed on, and he couldn't help thinking she still had a great body.

She pulled her hair back with an elastic band and started for the pool. "How has Duffy managed it for more than ten years?"

"One day at a time. Just the way we're doing it."

"Lord, give me strength," Sharon sang.

"That's one of the first steps ... learning there's a power greater than yourself."

"Jesus Christ, kid. Lighten up!"

She walked around the pool to the diving board, his eyes following her every step of the way. Her color was returning, and although she had lost too much weight, her hips and breasts still appeared generous in the clinging suit.

"You look better today."

"Really?"

"You're starting to look like the old Sharon Grant."

"Old?"

"Not old. I mean, you look great."

She turned back to him and with an impish smile asked, "Sexy?"

"Sexy as hell."

She laughed. "Guess you're not such a bad kid after all."

"I'm no kid."

"I'm becoming more and more aware of that, kiddo." She bounced up and down on the tip of the board a few times, dove into the water, and swam the crawl for six laps. Then she paddled over to the side of the pool near his feet to catch her breath.

"How do you feel?" he asked.

"Horny."

"That's the first thing you notice when you stop drinking. You're suddenly horny again," Brandon said, turning back to his stale, matter-of-fact law books.

"So that's all? I was beginning to think you were turning me on." The edge of the pool hid her mouth, but he saw her eyes were laughing.

"I wish I were," Brandon said under his breath.

"Forget it, kiddo. I'm old enough to be your mom."

"Yeah, right."

She spit a mouthful of water at him, hitting the bottoms of his feet.

"Hey!" he shouted.

She laughed and swam to the shallow end. As she climbed out of the pool, she let her hair down, snatched the beach towel from her chaise, and dried her arms and legs. "Kid, are you even dating anyone?"

He looked up at her, "You mean, a girl?"

"I sure as fuck hope so."

"Not really."

"Don't you like to fuck?"

He gave her a small, noncommittal shrug.

"Oh, good God, what's the world coming to? When I was your age, all guys could think of was fucking!"

"Fucking's okay." He put his book on the table next to the chaise.

"You're the master of understatement, kiddo!"

"I mean, you can fuck anyone."

"Anyone? I guess. Hey, you're not gay, are you?"

"No way."

"Alright. I only say that because I can tell you're one good lay." Sharon wondered if she was making the kid uncomfortable, so she changed the subject. "God, I'm famished. What time is it?"

"You mean, you relate to time?"

She laughed. "I'm beginning to. That's another thing about sobriety. You realize time marches on."

He looked at his watch. "You're not kidding. It's almost 1:00. Those cops will be here any minute."

She pulled a terrycloth robe over her shoulders, smirking. "Christ, life is so wonderful now! You won't let me drink or smoke dope, you're embarrassed to talk about sex with me, and the only dicks I'm allowed to see are fucking cops!"

———

Matthew Baldwin sat at his desk waiting for Jennifer Duffy to return his call. To pass the time, he methodically ripped a paper napkin into narrow strips, rolling them one by one into paper balls, which he lined up on his desk top in precise little rows. The napkin came with the Mocha Valencia he'd had his secretary pick up at the Starbucks in the lobby of his building.

Baldwin was always a picker-aparter of things when he had nothing better to do. The summer he was eight, he'd sat for hours on the back porch of his mother's flat in San Francisco, catching flies in flight with his quick little hands. After picking off their wings, he'd release them on the floor. He enjoyed the power of watching the creatures hop about, trying to fly, before he squashed them with his foot. His mother caught him at it one day and reprimanded him sternly, her mouth so close to his nose he could smell the sauerkraut she'd eaten for lunch. She whined that it was the work of the devil to mutilate or kill any of God's creatures for no good purpose. To show his contempt for her and her sermon, he popped a live fly into his mouth and ate it. She dragged him to her bedroom, pulled down his pants and whipped him with her tooled leather belt. Baldwin knew his mother hated him from the day he was born, as if he and the pain he'd brought her were not the work of the Lord, but that of the devil. The feeling was mutual.

The phone on his desk rang and his secretary announced Jennifer Duffy was on line two.

"My maid said you'd called," Jen said.

"I've some news for you."

"Good or bad?"

"A little of both."

"That's such a cliché."

"You husband says he has an alibi."

"You're kidding? Why didn't he tell me?"

"He spent that weekend with Sharon Grant, just a few blocks from your home."

"Impossible. He was at the cabin that night. I called him

there around 9:00 and again the next morning."

"Ever hear of call forwarding?"

"The bloody fool!"

"You should be ecstatic. If he was with Sharon Grant, he's off the hook."

"Oh, my God! That's why the silly twit's been acting so guilty. The bugger was cheating on me! I never imagined he had the balls to do it."

"Of course, he may be lying. I have to check it out with her."

"And if she says it's true?"

"I guarantee your husband will never be indicted."

———

Hicks and Torres had to ring the doorbell at the Seaman home four times before a tall young man in a terrycloth robe answered the door.

"Sorry," he said, "we were in back by the pool. I didn't hear the bell at first."

Hicks flashed him his shield. "I'm Lieutenant Hicks and this is Detective Torres. I talked to you earlier."

"Right. We've been expecting you."

Cash led them to the kitchen, where Sharon Grant was fixing herself a peanut butter and jelly sandwich. Her robe hung loosely around her shoulders, revealing the skin-tight bathing suit and her long, tanned legs. "Ah, the pigs have arrived."

Hicks was surprised by her appearance. He'd expected her face to be drawn and pale, but she was radiant.

"I'm Lieutenant Hicks. This is Detective Torres."

Torres gave her his most macho grin. "I'm a great admirer of yours, ma'am."

She took a bite from her sandwich. "Forget that bullshit. Think of me as just plain old Sharon. Please sit. Unless, of course, you're going to grill me standing up."

They all sat down around the table in the kitchen sunspace.

Hicks adjusted his glasses and began flipping through his notebook. But Sharon fired first. "Do you have any idea who killed Sam?"

Hicks shook his head. "That's what I was about to ask you."

"I'm clueless." She fished a pack of cigarettes from the pocket of her robe. "I must admit, of course, I considered it more than once." She lit a cigarette. "Just joking, of course."

"Did he have any enemies?" Hicks asked.

"Everyone has enemies, Lieutenant," she said, curling a long leg under her. "Sam had more than his share, but I can't think of anyone who'd even consider murdering him."

Hicks turned to Cash. "Did you know Mr. Shelton?"

"Brandon barely knew him," Sharon answered for him.

"Is that a fact, Brandon?" Hicks said.

"He was a fucking asshole."

"Brandon!" she scolded.

"I hated him."

Hicks looked at him over his glasses. "Enough to kill him?"

"That's a bullshit question!" she snapped, snuffing out the cigarette on her plate. "Brandon was here with me the night of the murder."

"You understand, Ms. Grant—"

"Sharon."

He nodded. "Sharon ... that I have to ask these questions."

"I suppose so. But you're not listening; I told you Brandon had nothing to do with it."

Hicks ignored her. "Any particular reason you hated Shelton?" he asked Cash.

"I didn't like what he was doing to Sharon."

"Brandon and Gordon thought Sam was turning me into an alcoholic."

"Was he?" Hicks asked.

"Yes," she admitted.

Hicks continued to dive into Sharon Grant's relationship with

Shelton. In the four years that they sort of lived together, he put quite a dent in her career—and her sanity. They drank too much and occasionally wrecked themselves with drugs. Shelton honed his Hollywood playboy reputation by throwing parties that often graduated into orgies that Sharon hated. But she wanted to please him, so she got as fucked up as she could and went with the flow. Everything she said seemed to confirm what Cash had just told them—Shelton was, in fact, an asshole.

"Did you love him?" Hicks finally asked.

"My shrink said I was fucking my father. Maybe I was. My Dad was twenty years older than my Mom. He died when I was in college. That could be why I've always been attracted to older men, but I was never really happy with Sam or anyone else." She smiled wistfully at Torres. "Maybe I should try my luck with younger guys."

"Maybe," Torres agreed, cocking an eyebrow.

Hicks asked, "Did you know Shelton had cancer?"

"What? Oh, God, no!"

"He may not have known. The autopsy showed he had cancer of the pancreas. Do you know if he took out any new insurance policies recently?"

"No. But Ginny would."

"Virginia Reed?" Hicks said.

She nodded. "Ginny handled all Sam's personal business. You should talk to her."

"I did. Yesterday," Torres said. "She said she thought Duffy murdered Shelton."

"Bullshit!" Cash flared.

Hicks asked. "You work for Mr. Duffy, don't you, Brandon?"

"Yes."

"And he sponsored you in AA?"

"Yes."

"How'd you meet?"

"I woke up on the floor one day and there he was."

Hicks was growing impatient with the kid. "Be serious."

"He is," Sharon said.

"My life was fucked up from the day I was born." Cash began. He confessed that he'd started to drink in middle school. His stepfather and mother separated when he was fifteen, and by time he graduated from high school, he was an alcoholic. He was smart, and his grades were good enough to get him into UCLA, but half way through his sophomore year, his stepmother was killed on the way to work in a seven-car pileup on the 405. The night of her funeral, he drank himself into a stupor in the back row of a Westwood movie theater. He woke up at the UCLA Medical Center where he had been in a coma for three days. Gordon Duffy was at his side when he finally came to. "He saved my life," Cash finished.

"Now he and Brandon are trying to save mine," Sharon added.

"So you both owe him a great deal, don't you?" Hicks flipped through the pages of his notebook, looked over his glasses at Cash. "Why did you call Mr. Duffy at his cabin Saturday afternoon the weekend of the murder?"

"Did I call him?" Cash asked.

Hicks nodded. "He claims you did."

"Then I guess I did."

"What did you talk about?"

Cash hesitated, before asking, "What did Mr. Duffy say?"

"I want to hear it from you."

Sharon interrupted, "Wasn't that the day I had the DTs so bad?"

Cash nodded. "Yeah. I took care of her all that weekend. She got very sick Saturday afternoon. Crazy sick, you know? So I called Mr. Duffy to see what I should do."

"And what did he say?" Hicks asked.

Cash hesitated. "That I could take care of it. He said the DTs were normal, and I should just pump her with fluids."

She stood up, tightening the sash of her robe. "And as you can see, he took very good care of me. Is that all Lieutenant?"

Hicks saw her eyes were glistening. Was she acting, or was she in worse shape than she appeared? "I don't have any more questions. How about you, Torres?"

"Just one." Torres grinned disarmingly. "Can you autograph a picture for me? I got a Polaroid camera in the car."

She seemed more relieved than flattered. "Sure. Go get your camera."

Hicks took a close-up of Torres and Sharon sitting at the kitchen table. She was beaming up at him, her right hand on his shoulder. Brandon was behind them, laughing. When it developed, Hicks looked at it, smiled, and handed it to her. She exclaimed, "Oh, my God! You can't see that I'm wearing a bathing suit under my robe!"

Torres looked at it and exclaimed, "Perfect!" He handed her his pen. "I'd love it if you'd sign it on the back."

She scribbled a line and her name on the back of the Polaroid and handed it to him. "How's that?"

Torres read it aloud, "To my favorite dick. Sharon Grant."

———

After Hicks and Torres left Geoffrey Seaman's home, Brandon Cash went back to his books on the patio. Sharon Grant had told him she was going to shower and take a nap, so when the phone on the patio rang he picked it up.

"Brandon Cash?" the voice on the line asked.

"Yes."

"Matthew Baldwin. I'm Gordon Duffy's attorney."

"Yes, sir?"

"Thought I'd better warn you. A homicide detective may be over there this afternoon to interview you and Ms. Grant—"

"Lieutenant Hicks, you mean? He just left a few minutes ago."

"What did you and Ms. Grant tell them?"

"I'm not sure I should tell you. Not until I've checked with Mr. Duffy."

"You're a law student, right? You should understand that I

can't help Mr. Duffy until I know all the facts."

"Uh, huh." Brandon rolled his eyes.

"Okay, now that we're on the same page, Mr. Duffy told me in strictest confidence that he wasn't at Big Bear the night of the murder. He claims he drove back to L.A. to help you with Ms Grant. Is that true?"

"Whatever."

"Brandon, if you want to help him ... was he with Ms. Grant and you in Bel Air the night of the murder?"

"If that's what he told you."

"Yes or no?"

Brandon sighed. "He was with Sharon."

"And that's what you told Lieutenant Hicks and the other detective this afternoon?"

"No. We told him what Mr. Duffy asked us to say: that he was up at the cabin at Big Bear the entire weekend."

"And that was a lie?"

"We weren't under oath."

"What the hell are they teaching you at UCLA? If you lie to an officer of the law when he's investigating a crime, it's a crime."

"I'm not sure that's true."

"Goddamn it, don't tell me about the fucking law! Now, let me talk to Ms. Grant."

"She's taking a nap, drying out, and she said she didn't want to be disturbed."

"Fine, but I need to talk to you both. I need everyone on the same wavelength. I'll come over there sometime around 6:00. You'll both be there, right?"

"I may not be here. Mr. Duffy said he'd relieve me later on this afternoon."

"I doubt that. I told him to stay away from Ms. Grant for a few days. Avoid any appearances of collusion. They teach you about that in law school yet?"

"I'll take care of her for a few days. No problem."

"Good. I'll see you both this evening."

21

Hicks and Torres were on their way to a 2:00 p.m. interview with Virginia Reed at the GameCo offices in Venice when Fahey called.

"Ben and I are just finishing up at the GameCo cabin," she reported. "We're finding mostly the kind of junk you'd expect to find at a weekend getaway place. There's just one computer. Crime lab techies are ghosting the hard drives, but they say there's not much there—mostly games and code writing software. He wasn't even connected to the Internet, and the phone had no answering machine. Guess Duffy really did want to get away from it all."

"Better trace the phone calls to and from the cabin the weekend Shelton was murdered."

"Already did. There were four calls to the cabin number that weekend. Three were from West L.A.; one at 5:37 p.m. from a Bel Air number listed to a Geoffrey Seaman, another from the Duffy residence at 8:26, and a third from a cell phone at 8:44, no name or number. Number four was another call from the Duffy residence at 9:14 Sunday morning."

"Duffy told me there were only three."

"He probably didn't remember the cell phone call. It only lasted just two seconds. The phone company says there's nothing unusual about the cabin's service; one line, and the only extras on it are call waiting and forwarding."

"You'd think a programmer would have DSL at least."

"Shit, there's not even a TV up here ... hey, hang on. Ben wants to give you the really big news."

Jackson's booming voice came on the line. "We had Harry Perz's brother take a look at the video and those two photos you faxed us. He crapped all over any case we might have against Duffy."

"He couldn't identify him?"

"Perz said the deputy he saw was much younger—late twenties, early thirties—and when we showed him your picture, he said that the perp wasn't as old or bald as you. But he did finger Shelton as the other guy in the car that sideswiped him."

"No shit?"

"Would I shit you, my man? Kinda ties the two cases together, don't it?"

"Depends on how reliable Perz is. For all we know, he's the perp."

"No way. The guy was on a trip that weekend. Red already checked with United."

"Okay, Ben. Put Fahey back on."

"Damn good news, right boss?"

"I'm not sure, Fahey. Something's not sitting right. I don't think Perz is a reliable witness."

"Come on! He's good as they get. What's hanging you up?"

"Ben said he said I was bald."

"Let's face it, boss. You are. That's what makes you so fucking sexy."

Hicks laughed. "Yeah, right. What about the dog? Any news there?"

"We have a vet digging for the slug. Haven't heard anything yet. Any idea when you and Torres will be back?"

"We're on our way to interview Shelton's secretary again. I'll check in with you when we're done."

———

GameCo's offices were in a restored three-story building overlooking Muscle Beach just south of 18th Avenue, built as a resort hotel shortly after Venice was founded on the Fourth of July in 1905. Since then, the landmark survived earthquakes, tsunamis, brief stints as a bordello, the headquarters for the U.S. Army Coastal Defense Command during War II, and a hippie hideaway for runaways and addicts.

Torres pulled into the parking lot at the rear of the GameCo building, and found the space marked "Mr. Shelton."

Torres grinned, pulled into the reserved spot, and said, "Hey, fuck 'em if they can't take a joke, right?"

Hicks ignored him as they climbed out of the Yukon, just in time to see a long-legged girl in a day-glo orange bra and a thong rollerblade past.

"Hicks, I got to get to Venice more often!" Torres said.

They walked around the building to GameCo's main entrance, merging into the flow of bathers, bikers, joggers, and strollers on Ocean Front Walk. Aging flower children lined the route, wandering in and out of drum circles, and hawking their beads and cheap, homemade incense. Across the walk from GameCo's entrance was a preserve of Schwarzenegger wannabes, lifting and pressing barbells, preening and flexing the well-oiled muscles that gave the beach its name. Hicks realized that the computer geeks fit in well.

Two thick glass doors were locked at the GameCo entrance. Torres put his hands against the glass to shade the glare and peered inside. A pretty young receptionist sat at her desk, smiling at him.

"Can I help you?" her voice came from the speaker beside the door.

Hicks took out his badge case and pressed it against the glass for her to see. "I'm Lieutenant Hicks of the San Bernardino—"

The locked handles buzzed, and the doors closed automatically behind them. The name plaque on the receptionist's desk identified her as Maria Moreno. Torres took one look at her and broke out his best on-the-make purr. "Hi, Maria."

"It's Mau-reea," she corrected him, but not unpleasantly.

"Like the island in Tahiti?" he asked.

She shook her head. "Like the seas on the moon."

"Oh?" He thought her black eyes sparkled like waves in the moonlight. "Well, my name's Torres," he said, rolling out the *r*. "Detective Torres—"

"Here about Mr. Shelton's murder, I bet," Maria finished for him. "Know who did it?"

"We have our suspects," Torres nodded, leaned on the mahogany, and changed the subject. "You like to rollerblade?"

Hicks cleared his throat for attention. "Virginia Reed's expecting us."

Maria picked up the phone and pushed a button on its console. "Two detectives are here to see you." She put down the receiver and smiled at Torres. "Ginny says she'll be down in a few minutes."

Hicks retreated to the couch, snatching the *L.A. Times* from the coffee table. Torres remained hunched over the reception desk. "Your parents gave you a very unusual name."

"Maria?" Maria smirked. "Are you a Taurus?"

"How'd you guess?"

"Because you're so full of it."

Virginia Reed stepped off the elevator and saw Torres first. She hurried over to him, extending her hand. "Detective Torres. So good to see you again."

Hicks put down the *Times* and got up from the couch. He hadn't noticed it over the phone, but now he thought he had heard Virginia Reed's voice before.

Torres shook her hand and turned toward Hicks as he strode up to them. "This is Lieutenant Hicks, ma'am."

Hicks said, "We have just a few more questions to ask you."

She nodded. "So you said when you called. Would you mind if we talked at Big Daddy's? I've been so busy, I haven't had any lunch. It's just a little way up the beach."

———

El Niño was gathering strength offshore for another swipe at Southern California as Hicks and Torres accompanied Virginia Reed up Ocean Front Walk to the café. They took a table on the veranda and ordered lunch, giving them a ringside view of the bizarre street show and its equally bizarre audience.

Virginia Reed seemed not to notice any of it. "So, how can I help you?"

Hicks asked, "We need to know when and where Mr. Shelton's funeral will be held."

She nodded toward the ocean. "Noon tomorrow. Right out there."

"You can't bury people on the beach ..." Torres said.

"No, no. Mr. Shelton prearranged his funeral with the Neptune Society about a year ago. His ashes will be sprinkled in the ocean a mile off the shore."

The fire-eater sprayed a fireball above the heads of the gawkers.

"That guy performing the cremation?" Torres asked.

Hicks frowned at him but Virginia laughed.

"Oh, I need a good laugh. GameCo's always been one big happy family. Now the office is as gloomy as a bank."

Hicks said, "Did you make the funeral arrangements?"

"No, I didn't know anything about them until Gordon called me last night. George Crawford, the senior partner of our legal firm, told him about the arrangements at a meeting they had Sunday afternoon. Mr. Crawford wrote the will, so he knew what Mr. Shelton's last wishes were."

"Did Mr. Shelton take out any new insurance policies recently?"

"Why would he? GameCo carried a five-million-dollar policy on him. Same with Gordon."

"The autopsy revealed Mr. Shelton had cancer of the pancreas. It probably would've been terminal within six months. "

"Then someone wasted a bullet." Virginia laughed, but she sounded nervous.

"What did you mean yesterday when you told detectives Fahey and Torres that Gordon Duffy deserved a kiss for killing Shelton?"

"Did I? Well, I didn't *actually* mean it. Really, Gordon—"

"You also told them Mr. Duffy had a motive."

"The stock agreement?" Torres reminded her.

Hicks said, "And who's the beneficiary of the five million dollar insurance policy?"

"GameCo. The stock holders are all beneficiaries."

"But Gordon Duffy had the most to gain?" Hicks said.

"Gordon did not murder Mr. Shelton. I know he didn't."

"That's not what you told me yesterday," Torres shot back.

"I was in shock. I was half kidding anyway."

"Did anyone ask you to change your story?" Hicks pressed.

"No."

Hicks' face hardened. "If you've any information that could help us solve Samuel Shelton's murder, and you don't reveal it to us, you could be charged as an accessory after the fact."

"Exactly what does that mean?"

"Jail time."

She let out a long sigh. "Sharon called me this morning. She wanted me to know Gordon couldn't possibly have murdered Mr. Shelton."

"She told us the same thing," Torres said.

"Then you know? I mean, how could he be the murderer if he was in Bel Air with Sharon?"

Hicks and Torres exchanged glances.

Virginia recognized that she'd said too much. The right side of her face sagged; and she closed her eyes, rubbing her temples. "Oh, dear, Sharon will never trust me again." She raised her handkerchief to her nose.

"It's been my experience that people don't tell secrets unless they want the truth to be known," Hicks said.

She thought about that for a moment and said, "Sharon and I have always been very close."

"How close?"

"She's my sister."

———

A street preacher jogged out of the crowd to the table where Hicks and Torres were sitting with Virginia Reed. He pirouetted twice, thrust a collection tambourine at them, shouting, "Praise the Lord!" Torres flashed him his badge, and the preacher recoiled, saying "The Lord be praised!" as he skated back into the crowd, pounding his tambourine.

The incident gave Hicks time to recover from Virginia Reed's bombshell.

"I should've guessed," he told her.

"Why? I'm fifteen years older than Sharon and we don't look a bit alike."

"You sound just like her," Hicks said as their lunch arrived. "So, Gordon Duffy was at Geoffrey Seaman's house?"

"I don't know whose house it is. But it's the place where she's staying now with Brandon."

"She could be lying to give Duffy an alibi."

"She'd never lie to me."

"Maybe, but it doesn't make sense," Hicks said. "Why would he tell me he was at the cabin if he had an alibi?"

"I honestly don't know."

"Was Duffy rubbing up on your sister?" Torres asked.

"Don't be ridiculous! There hasn't been anything between them in years."

"But there was once?" Hicks asked.

"It was so long ago. They're just friends now, but I think Gordon may be afraid Jennifer would use any excuse to walk out on him. Or maybe he's protecting Brandon."

"Protecting him from what?" Hicks asked.

She leaned forward to explain. "Sharon was just a kid when she got pregnant, not quite eighteen. She met Gordon when he was the special effects and computer animation director at Hodgepodge Productions. I was their production assistant. One of my jobs was to set up casting sessions. Sharon was a struggling young actress. I brought her in to try out for a commercial. We didn't want anyone to know she was my sister, so we changed her name."

"That's when Sharon Grant was born?" Hicks said.

She nodded. "It was her big break. She got the job and Gordon directed the spots. That was back in his drinking days. She was young, and he was a charmer like so many drunks seem to be. They had an affair, and she got pregnant. We were Catholic, so abortion was out of the question. Sharon had the baby, and I found him a home with a married friend who couldn't have kids."

"A friend named Cash?" Hicks asked.

"And you probably know the rest. He was a real problem kid; a junkie and alcoholic while he was still in high school. When he ended up in a coma at UCLA, I had to tell Gordon that Brandon was his son. Gordon had been in AA for years. If anyone could help the boy it was him."

"Were Sharon and Brandon ever aware of their relationship?"

"Neither of them know. They both had problems, and we didn't think they could handle the truth."

22

After lunch, Hicks and Torres left Virginia Reed at the GameCo office. Before they reached the employee parking lot in back of the building, it began to pour. They ran the last half block to Hicks' SUV.

"I've had it with this El Niño bullshit!" Torres grumbled as they climbed into the Yukon.

Hicks wiped his face with his handkerchief. "Never complain about rain when you live in Southern California. So, what's your take on all this, Torres?"

"I think we should trade this heap in on a fucking boat!"

"Seriously."

"I still think Duffy's the perp."

"Convince me."

"They're all lying to protect him. Personally, I don't give a good fuck where he was on the night of the murder. He didn't have to actually pull the trigger. He could've hired someone to do it."

"The perp's MO doesn't fit a professional hit."

"So, how could he be in two places at the same time? I mean, we know he made calls from the cabin three or four times that weekend. The phone company records prove it."

Hicks fished out his cell phone and dialed Fahey's number. "Hi,

Fahey. You and Ben back at the office yet?"

"Yeah. Where the fuck are you?"

"Still in Venice. And it's pouring. You still got the phone company print out of the calls from the cabin?"

"Right in front of me."

"Check the codes after the time and the place of each call."

Fahey dug for the phone records. "Holy, shit! Duffy was at the cabin when he answered the 5:37 call Saturday evening; but the other calls have an f next to them—they were forwarded from the cabin. Hicks? Do you know where he was?"

"With Sharon Grant in Bel Air."

"So he's got a fucking alibi?"

"Sure looks like it. But Torres still thinks Duffy murdered Shelton."

"Well, I've got some news. A vet recovered the slug from the dog. FEU says it's a .38 reload with six lands and six grooves. Same type that killed Shelton. That sure as hell ties all three homicides together."

Hicks thought it over for a moment before he asked, "Think Perz's brother could ID the perp if he saw him again?"

"He already fingered Shelton."

"I've got a shot of a possible suspect. It's a little too fuzzy to fax you. You and Ben pick up Perz and drive him down to L.A. I'd like to see how good his memory really is."

"He has a flight that gets into LAX at 9:20. Why don't Ben and I pick him up and drive him down there?"

"Great. And arrest him as a material witness if you have to."

"Okay, boss. Where do we meet you?"

"How about the Century Plaza Hotel coffee shop? Know where it is?"

"Yeah. In Beverly Hills. Just a couple of blocks from Shelton's apartment."

"Okay. Call me with your ETA after you've picked up Perz."

Hicks hit the end button and slipped the cell phone back in his pocket.

"What's the bullshit about us having a picture of the suspect?" Torres asked.

"Just don't lose that Polaroid I took of you and Sharon."

"Jesus! You think_"

"Yeah. Let's go."

"Where to? Bel Air?"

"No, West Hollywood. We need a little help from the L.A. Sheriff's Department."

———

The City of West Hollywood is sandwiched between Beverly Hills and Hollywood.   Below the Hollywood Hills, Santa Monica Boulevard was fast becoming a river. Torres turned onto San Vicente and drove a block south to the Sheriff's Department.

"I need Duffy's .38," Hicks said to Torres.

Torres reached under his seat where he had stashed the plastic evidence bag containing the revolver and handed it to Hicks. "You're not turning it in to them, are you? This is our entire case. Don't let these L.A. assholes cut in on us."

"They won't. But I need the reloads and the spent slugs you confiscated this morning, too."

Torres took the baggies containing the slugs and reloads from his jacket pocket. "Want me to tag along?"

"No, stay here." He handed Torres his cell phone. "Fahey's going to call when they're on their way here with Perz. Besides, there's no sense us both getting soaked."

Hicks leaped into the deluge. His left foot missed the curb and stepped into the white-water rapids gushing down the gutter. Clutching the evidence bags in his right hand, and the lapels of his jacket with his left, he sprinted to the entrance. His shoes squeaked, leaving puddles behind as he crossed the polished floor to the front desk.

"What can I do for you, sir?" the uniformed male receptionist asked.

"I'm Homicide Lieutenant Hicks, San Bernardino Sheriff's Department. I need some help."

The receptionist examined his credentials. "What can we do for you?"

"I need ballistics tests on these." Hicks held up the evidence bags.

The receptionist grinned. "I didn't think San Bernardino was that far out in the sticks. Don't you have your own lab?"

Hicks smiled, but his voice had an annoyed edge to it. "I need the tests done right this minute. I'm trying to wrap up a murder investigation."

"I'll see what I can do. In the meantime, there's a men's room down there if you'd like to dry off."

Hicks took the evidence bags to the men's room and put them in one of the wash basins while he dried his face and hands with paper towels. When he was finished, he removed his left shoe and sock. He wrung out the sock, and then he put it and the shoe back on and returned to reception.

A stocky Asian man with a wispy gray Fu Manchu was waiting for him by the desk.

"Lieutenant Hicks? Fred here said you looked like a drowned rat." He extended his hand to
Hicks. "Tad Oki. Tad's short for Tadori, but around here, everyone calls me Okey-Dokey. Understand you got a gun and a problem?"

Hicks handed him the evidence bag. Oki took one look at the revolver in the bag and said, "Thirty-eight Smith & Wesson." He grinned at Hicks. "Anything else I can help you with?"

"We took a slug out of a body up at Big Bear. I need to know if it came from this gun."

"No problem." Oki led Hicks down the hall. "Got the murder slug?"

"That's the problem. Slug's at our FEU lab."

"Still no problem if your lab's on the net."

"It is."

They took the stairs to the basement. It took Oki less than half an hour to complete the first part of the test. He slipped three of Duffy's reloads into the .38 and after he and Hicks donned ear protections, fired them into a tub of water. They took high-resolution digital pictures of them and half a dozen of the deformed .38 reloads Torres had confiscated that morning from the coffee can in Duffy's basement workshop.

While Oki prepared his specimens, Hicks called the FEU lab in San Bernardino to request digital images of the slugs taken from Shelton and from Perz's dog.

The FEU man told Hicks, "I've also got some info for you on the weapon. Detective Torres phoned us the serial number a couple of hours ago. The .38 was registered to some Berkeley cop who was killed back in '89 when he ran his black-and-white into a tree trying to avoid a deer. Happened in the hills above the UC campus. Someone lifted his weapon before the emergency vehicles arrived on the scene."

"The gun's hot?"

"Hot as a gun can get. Berkeley PD says it was used in a Bay Area drive-by six months after it was lifted. Some old lady got blown away. Doesn't make much sense, does it? Why would someone like Duffy have a hot gun in his collection?"

"Beats me, but I'll sure as hell ask him the next time we talk."

"Okay. Tell your guy I'm downloading the slugs."

A few minutes later, Oki began comparing them with the digital images he'd made. Hicks hovered over his shoulder as he spent the better part of another twenty minutes examining and analyzing the slugs' striations.

"Well," Oki said, "I hate to disappoint you, Lieutenant. But the murder slug and the one from the dog did not come from the weapon you brought in. They may have six lands and six grooves, but the striations are nowhere near a match."

"You're absolutely sure?"

"But you're half right," Oki continued.

"About what?"

"Some of the slugs in your baggies matched the slugs from the .38 you brought in; and some of them matched the slugs that came from the victim and the dog."

The rain had stopped, but the clouds still looked threatening when Hicks climbed back into the Yukon.

"Jesus Christ!" Torres said as Hicks slid onto the seat next to him. "What took so long? I was beginning to think the fuckers were holding you for ransom."

"Sorry," Hicks said, fastening his seatbelt, "but I just had a very interesting hour and a half."

"That makes two of us. Fahey called. She says things are getting creepy. She and Ben are on the way down here with Perz. They'll be here by 6:30; the rain has all the freeways fucked up." Torres looked at his watch. "So that gives us an hour, maybe more, to kill. Where to now?"

"Duffy's place."

Torres started the SUV and put it in gear. "I knew it! That .38 was the murder weapon, right?"

"No. Ballistics just proved it wasn't." Hicks filled Torres in as they drove to Bel Air.

"Jesus Christ!" Torres said when he finished. "This gets weirder and weirder. Duffy's gun is hot, but it's not the murder weapon, but some of the slugs I fished out of the coffee can in the basement match the murder bullets? It's fucking unbelievable!"

A few minutes later, the Yukon turned into the Duffy's driveway. They went up the front steps and rang the bell. The Duffy's maid, Margarita, opened the door.

"*Buenos tardes,*" Torres said, charming the gatekeeper. "*Me recuerdas?*"

"*Sí,*" Margarita said. "Detective Torres."

"*Sí, señora. Y este es mi supervisor, Leniente Hicks. Queremos hablar con el señor Duffy.*"

"*Un momento, por favor, necesito saber si se poderia hablar contigo.*" She closed the door, leaving them looking back down the front steps.

Torres grinned at Hicks. "How do you like that?"

"She's a little heavy for you, isn't she?"

"I don't mean the maid," Torres said. "My Spanish. It's bad ass, right?"

"Muy malo," Hicks said straight-faced. "You speak about as well as the President."

"You mean *Presidente*."

The door opened and Gordon Duffy didn't wait for any niceties. "My attorney advised me not to answer any of your questions unless he's present," he said.

"We don't need to ask you any questions," Hicks lied. He held up the plastic bag that contained Duffy's .38. "We just want to return your gun. Ballistics proved it's not the murder weapon."

"Why, thank you," Duffy said, more than a little surprised, "I was sure of that."

Hicks nodded. "It's also not your gun."

"It's not the gun your detective picked up this morning?"

"Oh, it's the weapon he took from your collection, all right," Hicks said. "But it's not your property. It was stolen from a Berkeley policeman who was killed in a car crash back in '89."

Duffy blinked at the gun in the baggie. "It was stolen?"

"And it has a homicide history. It was used to blow away a woman in a San Francisco drive-by shooting years ago."

Duffy turned the plastic bag over in his hands. "How could that be? It's one of my first guns. I've had it almost twenty years."

"Do you have the registration number?" Hicks asked.

"Of course, in my computer."

"Those numbers probably don't match this gun's numbers."

"I don't understand. If this isn't my gun, how'd it get in my collection?"

"Anyone else in your household have access to the collection?" Hicks asked.

"The cabinet's always locked."

"The lock's a piece of shit," Torres said. "I opened it without a key."

"Who has access? Your maid? Your wife?" Hicks asked.

"I suppose you could say Margarita has access to it," Duffy said. "I unlock it for her about once a month so she can dust. My wife hates guns."

Hicks asked, "What about your son?"

"Son?" Duffy whispered, stunned.

"We know all about Brandon," Hicks said, his voice hardening. "Now, I don't give a shit what your lawyer told you; you'd better invite us in and explain a few things."

23

Mathew Baldwin left his office early that afternoon. He told his secretary he'd be doing research on the Duffy case and that he probably wouldn't be in the rest of the afternoon.

By the time Baldwin turned off Sunset Boulevard onto Doheny Road, the heavy downpour was letting up; and he could see patches of blue and an occasional ray of sunshine through breaks in the scud. He drove three blocks west, passing the rows of towering high-rises overlooking Beverly Hills, and pulled into the underground garage of his building. He removed a nylon athletic duffel from the trunk of his Lexus and took the elevator to the tenth floor.

Entering his apartment, he shouted, "Mother, I'm home!"
He passed through the living room on his way to the utility room off the kitchen. Opening the sports duffel, he emptied the dirty sweats and socks he'd worked out in the day before into the washing machine, turned it on, and carried the duffel back through the living room to the master bedroom suite.

"No, mother," he yelled just to bug her, as he always did when passing the place where she always sat, "I didn't take my medicine today."

He tossed the sports duffel on the bed, went into the bathroom, opened the medicine cabinet and took out a prescription bottle of Depakote. Lifting the lid of the toilet with one foot, he poured the pills into the bowl.

He returned to the living room, crossed to the Italian marble fireplace and stood there, grinning at an antique Chinese porcelain urn on the mantle. He'd decided the urn was the perfect gift for his mother the moment he spotted it in the antique gallery of San Francisco's Sir Francis Drake Hotel. The urn's dark blue background was overlaid with delicate white carnations. Carnations were his mother's favorite flowers, so, naturally, he hated them. To him, a white carnation was the face of death itself.

When Baldwin was a child, his mother made him wear a red carnation on their annual Mother's Day pilgrimages to his grandmother's grave at Holy Cross Cemetery on the slopes of San Bruno Mountain just south of San Francisco. The red carnation told the world his mother was alive. She, of course, always wore a white carnation as a sign her mother was dead.

"Did you hear me mother?" he asked the urn.

He removed the lid and lifted it to his ear, the way a child holds a seashell to listen to the sound of waves. He smiled when he heard nothing. "Did you fucking hear me, mother?" he yelled into the ashes. "I said *fuck*! What about that? Huh? Fuck you!" He carried the urn into the bathroom and poured some of its contents into the toilet. He had to flush it five times before the water completely cleared.

He put the urn back on the mantle. Returning to the bedroom, he changed out of his suit into more casual clothes. He stuffed the sports duffel with a fresh set of gym clothes, two bath towels, and a prescription bottle containing fifty temazepam fifteen-milligram capsules. He zipped up the bag, grabbed a lightweight rain poncho off a hook in the hall closet, and took the elevator down to the garage.

He spent the next hour working out at the West Hollywood Athletic Club.

―――

Baldwin took a long, hot shower after his workout and got dressed. He took the prescription bottle of temazepam from his duffel bag, and tossed it into a second duffel; a heavier one he kept in his gym locker. On his way to Bel Air, he stopped at a convenience store on Santa Monica Boulevard to pick up gifts for Sharon and Brandon. He cruised past Geoff Seaman's home twice before he pulled into the curving brick drive, parking in the shadows of the high night-blooming jasmine bushes. He turned on the overhead lights and pulled the rearview mirror toward his face. He stared into his own eyes, counting backwards from one hundred.

At eighty-two, he grabbed the sports duffel from the passenger seat, climbed out, and stood in the shadows, surveying the house and yard. Towering eucalyptus, royal palms, and hedges of bamboo and shrubs completely curtained off the property from neighboring homes. Geoffrey Seaman valued his privacy. Sucking in his breath, he started up the walk to the front door, marveling at how fresh and sweet the rain-washed air tasted.

He pressed the doorbell and heard the chimes inside. The door was opened by a young man in jeans and a UCLA sweatshirt. Baldwin smiled, extending his hand. "You must be Brandon. I'm Matt Baldwin." Cash shook his hand. "I really apologize for barging in on you like this," Baldwin said, following Cash down the hall, "but what I have to do can't wait."

"That's okay," Cash said, "I've been studying for my finals all afternoon and Sharon's been up for an hour. We both could use a break."

Sharon Grant was in the kitchen pouring herself a third cup of coffee when they came in. She smiled and tightened the sash of her robe. "Mr. Baldwin, I presume?" she said, reaching for the sugar. "Sorry I'm so out of it. I've had a fuck of a time lately." Sharon stuck her hand out for Baldwin.

He took it, beaming, as if her touch were pure pleasure. "I hope you won't think me forward if I tell you that you look even more beautiful in real life."

"You're very kind," she said, slipping her hand from his and fishing out a pack of cigarettes from the pocket of her robe.

"Not kind," he said. "Truthful."

"The truth is, I'm a fucking mess. You know it and I know it, so let's cut the bullshit." She lit a cigarette and picked up her coffee mug and carried it to the round table in the sunspace. "Sit," she said, taking the chair on the window side of the table. "You, too, kiddo."

Brandon took the chair next to her and Baldwin sat opposite them, placing the sports duffel on the floor.

"Beautiful evening," he said. "El Niño really cleared out the smog."

"Thanks to global warming," Cash said.

Baldwin smiled. "So I've been told. But it's not exactly warm out there, and they're forecasting more rain. So much for sunny California."

"It was fucking beautiful this morning," Sharon said, blowing out a stream of smoke. She took a sip from her mug. "Would you like a cup of coffee?"

"No, thanks. I'm coffeed out."

"So am I. But I drink it anyway ... way too much." She drew on the cigarette, and smoke trailed out of her mouth as she spoke. "I smoke too much too, but what the hell, you can't quit everything all at once, right?"

"Right," Baldwin agreed.

"We've got Coke and Perrier," Cash told him.

"No thanks," he said again. "But you know what I could really use? A good stiff drink," he said with a wry smile.

Sharon and Cash exchanged glances.

"Scotch or vodka will do," Baldwin said.

She cocked her head, giving him an icy stare and snuffed out her cigarette in an ashtray. "Sorry. But there's not a drop in the house." Her eyes darted to Cash. "Right, kiddo?"

"Not a drop."

"Alright, then." Baldwin raised the sports duffel to his lap and took out a 1.7 liter bottle of Lauder's scotch, placing it on the table. "I thought this might be a BYOB affair."

Sharon's face flushed.

"Oh, you don't drink scotch? I should've known. Lots of people hate the taste." He reached in the duffle again and placed a liter of Popov next to the scotch.

"Are you out of your goddamn mind? She told you we don't drink!" Cash flared, jumping to his feet.

Sharon pulled him back down by his sleeve and flashed Baldwin a nervous smile. "Maybe you don't understand. We're recovering alcoholics."

"Well then, shit, you must be dying for a drink," Baldwin unscrewed both caps and tossed them over his shoulders.

"Get your fucking ass and those bottles out of here!" Sharon ordered.

"But I just got here. And it *is* the cocktail hour." Baldwin held the open bottle to his nose. "Mmm, that smells good! Even if it is the cheap shit." He thrust the bottle under Sharon's nose, booze splashing on the table in front of her. "Take a whiff."

She turned her head away. "Throw him out, Brandon!"

Cash rose from his chair again, fists clenched. Baldwin pulled a .38 from the bag and pointed it at him. Sharon screamed. Cash slowly sank back onto his chair, his eyes frozen on the gun.

"Well, I'm sure now you'd both like a drink," Baldwin said. "On the rocks? Neat?"

"We don't drink." Cash picked up the vodka bottle and began to pour it out. Baldwin squeezed the .38's trigger. There was a brilliant flash from the muzzle silencer followed by a sharp, zipping sound. The bottleneck and the tip of Cash's index finger were blown through the glass of the window behind him.

———

Baldwin allowed Sharon to get a pile of clean dishtowels from a drawer in the kitchen.

"Shit! Shit!" Cash gasped, squeezing his finger. "The whole fucking tip's gone."

"You're lucky I'm Mr. Nice Guy," Baldwin taunted. "I could've blown your arm off."

"We've got to get him to a hospital!" she pleaded, searching his face for any sign of why this was happening to them.

"Pour a little scotch on it and wrap it up. Don't be such a pussy. And watch your mouth!"

"You're fucking crazy!" Brandon said.

"Yes, mother," Baldwin returned with a smirk. He got up from table and took a couple of glasses from a cupboard, placing them on the table next to the bottles of liquor.

Sharon was choking down sobs, tying a dishtowel around Brandon's arm to make a tourniquet. Intuitively, she realized the facts. "You killed Sam, didn't you?" she cried. "And now you want to kill us."

"Wrong!" Baldwin shouted, sliding back onto his chair. "I just want to treat you two to a drink." He began filling the glasses with vodka.

"You can't make us drink," Cash groaned.

"Untrue! Drink up. Or I'll blow your fucking fingers off, one by one."

24

Gordon Duffy led Hicks and Torres upstairs to his home office. While the detectives watched from the opposite side of his desk, he opened a file in his computer and checked the serial numbers of his collection.

"I'll be damned. The numbers don't match," he finally said.

"Can you explain that?" Hicks asked.

"Now, look," Duffy stammered, "I know what you think. That I murdered Sam ... then switched guns and got rid of the murder weapon—"

"You're no longer our primary suspect," Hicks cut him off. "We know you weren't at Big Bear the night of the murder. You were just down the street ... here in Bel Air with Sharon Grant."

"Who told you that?"

"Virginia Reed," Torres said.

Hicks said, "You're aware of Grant's and Reed's relationship?"

"Yes, they're sisters."

"And you and Sharon are Brandon's parents?"

"Yes, but they don't know it. I never told them."

"Brandon's a pretty smart kid, isn't he? I mean, being a law student and all."

Duffy nodded.

"Then it's possible he knows that you're his father, isn't it? He could have learned who he really is by checking L.A. county's records? Adoption records aren't as secret as they used to be. If an adoptee wants to find his real parents, most courts now agree the kid has the right to know." Hicks said.

"And law students know their way around courthouses," Torres added.

"No," Duffy insisted, "it wouldn't be that easy for Brandon. He was born in Wisconsin and Sharon spent the last three months of her pregnancy with her grandmother in Milwaukee. We told Sharon that Brandon was put up for adoption there, but Ginny brought him back to L.A. and put him up for adoption here."

"Was your name on his birth certificate?"

"I don't know. I never saw it."

"If your name was there, it's possible he knows you're his father. Right?"

"I don't know. I suppose so." Duffy said.

"Do you have a will?"

"Of course."

"Is Brandon mentioned in it?"

"Yes. He'll share my estate with my wife, Jennifer."

"Does your wife know that?"

"No. I never told her about Brandon. And she doesn't know all the details of my will."

"Why didn't you tell her?"

"It's a long story ..."

"I'm sure it is," Hicks said. He took the baggie with the spent .38 slugs from his jacket pocket. "Detective Torres found these in a coffee can in your basement workshop. We ran ballistic tests on them. Some of the slugs have striations that match the weapon I just returned to you. A few of the others match the striations on the murder slug. They definitely didn't come from the same weapon."

"Are you sure?"

"Positive. How do you explain that?"

Duffy put a hand to the back of his neck and shook his head. "I can't."

"I think I can," Hicks went on. "Somebody in this household has been practicing with both weapons down in your target range."

"How is that? If someone were practicing down there, my wife or I would have heard it."

"You both work all day, don't you?"

"But Margarita would have heard. She's here every day except Wednesday and Thursday."

"When you met us at the front door, I only asked you about your wife and your maid. What about Brandon?"

"Brandon? No way."

"He lives above your garage. You said he's your handyman, so he must have access to the house."

"Brandon had nothing to do with this."

"He sure hates the shit out of Samuel Shelton," Torres said.

"Shelton really did a number on his mom ..." Hicks added.

"Look, Brandon's a nice, gentle kid—"

"But pretty much a loner, right?" Hicks said.

"What's that got to do with anything?"

"Most serial killers are loners," Torres said.

"Serial killer? I thought we were talking about Sam."

"Whoever murdered Mr. Shelton also murdered two other people that night."

"Oh, God, no!"

Hicks sat forward in his chair and his voice took on a hard edge. "Did you ask Sharon Grant to lie about your whereabouts the weekend of the murder?"

"Yes."

"And Brandon?"

"Yes."

"Why? Who were you protecting?"

"Look, I just didn't want my wife to know where I really was."

"I'm warning you, Mr. Duffy, stop asking people to cover your ass. Solving murders isn't easy, and you haven't made my job easier by fucking around with my witnesses. Do it again, and you'll find yourself behind bars for obstruction of justice. Got it?"

"I won't do it again."

"Do what again?" Jennifer Duffy's angry voice interrupted from the doorway.

"Sorry, ma'am," Hicks said, as he and Torres rose to their feet. "We were just asking your husband a few questions."

"You're sorry?" She stalked into the room and pointed toward the door. "Get out!"

"Jen, they're just—"

"Gordon!" she cut him off. "Your attorney told you not to talk to them unless he's present."

"They know I'm not a suspect."

Torres flashed his most appealing grin. "We just returned his gun, ma'am. It's not the murder weapon."

"Get out of my house!" she shouted.

"Does your wife know about your relationship with Brandon?" Hicks asked Duffy.

She turned on her husband, "You're having a *relationship* with that child above our garage?"

Hicks turned to Torres. "We'd better go."

As he and Torres hurried down the long, circular staircase, they heard Jennifer Duffy shouting at her husband. "You brought a bloody poofter into my house?"

25

Torres pulled into the circular drive of the Century Plaza Hotel shortly after 6:00 p.m. and parked in the loading zone just beyond the entrance, flipping down the driver's side sun visor to display the Sheriff's Department ID.

When he and Hicks climbed out, one of the doormen hurried up to them, waving his hand, unaware of the shield on the visor. "If you're checking in, leave the keys in the car."

Hicks flashed his ID at him. "We're here on official business, and there'll be another carload of deputies arriving any minute. Tell them we're in the coffee shop."

Hicks and Torres took a corner booth in the coffee shop that was set up for six without waiting for the hostess to seat them. They were studying their menus when she rushed up.

"Sorry," she said, "but we're awfully busy this evening. Would you mind moving to a smaller booth or table?"

Torres held up his badge. "More of us coming."

"Oh, I am sorry," she said, sounding like she really meant it this time.

Hicks started ordering. "I'd like a steak sandwich, medium rare, French fries, salad with the house dressing and a glass of milk ..."

As he closed his menu, the hostess said, "I'll get your waitress."

"We're in a real hurry, ma'am," Torres said, smiling, reaching out and grasping her hand. "Hot on the trail of a serial killer. He's even shot a dog ... you understand."

"Well, I suppose I could take your order, then," she gave in.

A waitress brought their order a few minutes later. They'd almost finished eating when Ben Jackson and Fahey brought Jerry Perz into the coffee shop.

"Ah, food!" Jackson boomed. "I'm starved!"

"What took you so long?" Torres asked.

"The freeways suck." Fahey said. She nodded at Perz. "This is Jerry Perz. Ben's driving scared him shitless."

Hicks extended his hand to him. "Understand you may be able to identify your brother's murderer."

"Sure hope I can help."

Hicks took out his notebook and showed Perz the Polaroid Torres had taken of Hicks and Sharon Grant. "See this guy in the background," he said, pointing at the fuzzy image of Brandon Cash standing behind them. "Could this be him?"

"Oh, wow, Sharon Grant!" Perz said. "You know her?"

"I'm her favorite dick," Torres said with a grin.

"Forget her," Hicks told Perz. "Recognize the guy standing behind us?"

"I don't know. He's not in focus. I mean, it was pretty dark that night." Perz hesitated. "But I'd know for sure if I could hear his voice. I'm real good at remembering voices."

"Jerry, would you mind sitting at another booth for a minute," Hicks said. "I don't want you to hear what I'm going to tell the other officers. It could compromise you as a witness."

"Can I order something to eat?"

"Sure," Hicks said, "anything you want. It's on me."

Hicks waited until Perz was out of earshot before he said, "The guy in the picture is a law student named Brandon Cash. He's the illegitimate son of Sharon Grant and Gordon Duffy—"

"No shit?" Fahey said.

"I don't have time to go into it now, but I believe Cash murdered Shelton, Harry Perz, and the Ricco woman."

"You agree, Torres?" Fahey asked.

"Hell, I thought it was Duffy all along. But then, I didn't know about the kid until this afternoon, so now I gotta go along with the boss. Cash seems like a good kid, but he is a loner, and he's overprotective of Sharon. So he fits the FBI's profile. Right?"

"Criminal Justice 101." Fahey said.

"All I know is, if I don't get some food in this gut, I'm gonna have a bitch of an ulcer," Jackson said rubbing his belly.

"Okay. Ben, you and Fahey stay here with Perz and get something to eat." Hicks scribbled an address on a page of his notebook, tore it out, and slid it across the table to Jackson. "Cash is babysitting Sharon Grant at this address in Bel Air. Torres and I will run over there now and interview them again. But this time, we'll tape it. When you guys finish dinner, drive over to join us, but keep Perz outside. When we finish the interview, we'll play the tape for Perz. If he recognizes Cash's voice, I'll schedule a line-up at the West Hollywood station. Let's handle this one by the book."

"Can I tag along with you guys?" Fahey said.

"Don't you want to eat?" Hicks asked.

"I'm on a diet," she said.

Torres laughed. "Bullshit. You just wanna meet Sharon Grant."

"Yeah, I wanna ask her why you're her favorite dick."

———

Sharon Grant and Brandon Cash were feeling no pain. They sat slumped in their chairs at the table in the sunspace of Geoffrey Seaman's house, which was slowly starting to spin. Baldwin sat opposite them, holding the .38 in his lap. Sharon hummed to herself like a child, making designs with her finger in the puddle of scotch that had spilled on the tabletop. Cash's chin rested on his chest, his eyes blinking stupidly at the bloody kitchen towel wrapped around his hand.

"More ice?" Baldwin asked cheerily, reaching into the icemaker container. He dropped a fistful of cubes into Cash's glass.

Sharon raised her eyes from the table and squinted at Baldwin, trying to bring him into focus.

"You know, this scotch is awful. The guy's a fucking attorney, ya' think he could afford some

fucking Macallan or something ... I can't drink any more."

"It's rotgut!" Cash agreed, straightening in his chair. He was pressing his left hand against the wall in an honest attempt to keep the room from tilting over on its side. "Really really really cheap!"

"Well, too fucking bad for you," Baldwin said. "I thought alcoholics didn't care what they drank. Hell, the cheap shit gets you just as drunk as the expensive stuff."

"I don' wanna get drunk. Period. I really don' wanna." Sharon bit her lower lip. "Oh, God! My lips are getting numb."

"Just like the good ol' days!" Baldwin said, filling Cash's glass to the brim.

"Fuck you," Cash said.

Baldwin shook his head disapprovingly. "Oh, Brandon. You definitely shouldn't swear in front of your mother."

Cash glared at him. "What the fuck did you say?"

"Don't swear in front of your *mother*," Baldwin repeated, slowly.

Sharon brushed aside the hair that was hanging in her face, turning toward Cash. "He's out of his fucking mind, kiddo."

Baldwin frowned at her. "What kind of example are you setting for your son? My mother never said bad words like that."

She giggled, and flopped into a chair. "Fuck your mother ... motherfucker."

Baldwin sighed. "That's the trouble with America today. Too many single moms don't have their act together. They drink too much, swear too fucking much ... and fuck anyone who spends more than five minutes with them."

"Drunk-cursing-fucking-mothers? Yeah, that's the world's biggest problem ..." Cash mumbled with a guffaw.

"This is the last time I'm going to warn you!" Baldwin snapped, pressing the .38's silencer against Cash's temple. "She's your mother! Don't talk like that in front of your mother!"

Sharon took another swallow from her glass and rolled her eyes. "You ... you think I'm kiddo's mom? No fucking way! Oh, God! He's my son? You're so full of shit ..."

Baldwin snapped, "Am I? Well, then it's time you two were introduced. Sharon Reed, meet your son, Brandon Cash—"

"You stupid fucking asshole. Her name is Grant!" Cash shouted staggering to his feet.

Baldwin cocked the .38's hammer. "Sit, or I'll blow you away."

Cash snorted at the gun and sank back on the chair.

"Grant's not your real name, is it Sharon?" Baldwin said.

She shook her head and looked over at Brandon. "It's just a stage name."

"You changed it a few months after your son was born."

"If you say so. I don't know anything for sure anymore, that sure is for fucking sure."

"But you had a son, didn't you?"

She fumbled for a cigarette, but her pack was empty. Crushing it into a ball, she dropped it on the floor, smiling at Baldwin. "Got a cigarette, dear?"

"I quit."

She shrugged. "Wish I could."

Brandon put his good hand on hers. "Sharon, did you have a son?"

She emptied her glass in a gulp, filled it with ice and held it to her forehead. "I don't know. It was a long, long time ago. So long ... I almost forgot about him."

Baldwin lowered her glass and refilled it. "But you do remember. You had a son."

She shook her head. "Kiddo can't be my kid ... my kid's in

Milwaukee. Right where I left the little pink bastard ... with my gramma and sister. I never saw him again." She put down her glass and studied Brandon's face, then started to cry uncontrollable, heaving sobs. "Oh, God, Brandon! Are you my baby?"

Cash pulled his hand away. "What? He's full of shit, Sharon."

"Oh, kiddo" she whispered, "I'm so sorry if I gave you away. I'll make it up to you, kiddo. I swear, I will."

Baldwin raised his own glass in a toast. "Drink up," he said cheerfully, sliding the open vodka bottle across the table. "Now you've both got something to really celebrate."

Cash leaned forward, squinting at her. "You're not my mother?" he half-asked, not comprehending.

Sharon sat up in her seat. "Well? Shit, kid. Is that so awful? I mean ... if I really am your mother?"

"Tell him who his father is," Baldwin ordered.

"Oh, God, I can't," she said, gripping the edge of the table.

"Tell him," Baldwin said, lifting the .38.

She wiped her mouth with her hand and mumbled.

"Stop being such a bad mother. Tell your son who his father is!" Baldwin ordered.

"Gordon!" she cried.

"What?" Cash asked.

Sharon nodded.

"And he knows?"

"I don't know," she said, shaking her head.

"The answer is: Correct! Yes, he knows," Baldwin said. "His will is on file at my office. I've seen it. And if you should live so long, Brandon, you get half his estate. Isn't that good news?" He reached into the duffel bag, took out the bottle of temazepam and poured half the capsules into the palm of his hand. "Okay, mommy," he said, offering her the handful of pills, "time to take your medicine."

Cash exploded, "You fucking son-of-a-bitch!" With all the strength that was left in him, he rammed the table into Baldwin's gut, catching the lawyer off balance. The pills flew out of his hand as he and his chair toppled over backwards.

Sharon screamed.

Cash staggered around the table. Baldwin lay sprawled on his back, the .38 still in his hand. He raised it and squeezed the trigger. There was a muffled pop, and the slug crashed into the upper left side of Cash's chest, throwing him backward against the wall. Slowly, he slid to the floor, his eyes round with amazement, staring at the red stain spreading across his sweatshirt.

"Oh, my God!" Sharon screeched, staggering toward Cash. "You shot kiddo! You shot my baby!"

Baldwin scrambled to his knees and began picking up the sleeping capsules scattered about the floor.

Sharon knelt beside Cash, wailing, "Oh, kiddo! Can you hear me? Baby?"

Baldwin rose to his feet, shoved the .38 into his belt, and grabbed a handful of her hair. When she opened her mouth to scream, he clapped the handful of pills into it and held it shut as he dragged her down the hall to the master bedroom.

26

Gordon Duffy invariably took his evening meal on a tray in the media room at the back of his house while he watched the NBC Nightly News—another of his habits that annoyed his wife.

Jen had been born and raised in Stockport, a grimy working class suburb of Manchester in England's industrial Midlands. Her father, Frank Frost, owned a small clothing factory. In the 40s and 50s, the factory turned out coveralls for the coal miners of Wales and the automobile workers of Birmingham and Coventry. When the mines and factories began closing in the 60s and 70s, he had enough foresight to see that his future lay in cranking out jeans for the kids. The Frost family was not rich, but was considered well off, and Jen grew up imagining herself a princess of sorts. When she got her A Levels in computing from nearby Preston College, she left the UK to seek her fortune in America. Now that she'd found it, and had the money to live like a princess, her prince was a middle-aged frog who acted and dressed like a commoner.

"Damn Duffy and his damned dinners in front of the TV!" she thought. She wondered what was the point of having a lovely formal dining room, beautiful linens, Royal Cauldon china and antique sterling silver if they were never used? And she hated him for having a son he'd never even mentioned, living above their garage! And Brandon—she would have preferred him to be Duffy's poofter lover than his bastard son. A bastard son could share her inheritance!

Somehow, she managed to control her temper and to apologize to Duffy for her outburst. Hadn't Matthew Baldwin told her to be nice to him, to butter him up, make him feel good, keep him at home that evening? She had ordered a special dinner for them that evening—lobster bisque, Caesar salad, poached salmon for the fish course, followed by roast duck in orange sauce and a chocolate mousse pie. She had personally gone down to their wine cellar to pick a special wine to be served with the dinner, a bottle of Dom Perignon, 1974, for herself and sparkling Catawba grape juice for him.

Jen wore the full-length black Hanae Mori gown she'd bought on their trip to the Tokyo Game Fair the year before. She'd asked her husband to dress for dinner, too, and because he was anxious to please her after their argument about Brandon, he gave up the news, and appeared at the dinner table in a three-piece corduroy suit.

Duffy was anything but happy as he slurped his soup by candlelight. "I'm sorry about Brandon," he said crossly.

"Don't be angry," Jen said. "It's over. I never should have acted the way I did. It's just ... that damn copper caught me off guard. I never dreamed Brandon was your son. Why did you keep it a secret from me? I'm your wife. I love you. I would have—"

"Really? Would you really have—" Duffy asked, growing emotional.

"Loved you enough to accept your son? Yes, Gordon. I would."

He inhaled another spoonful of bisque. "I don't know what I thought."

"Well, now you know, luv." She sipped her champagne. "I think it's time we moved Brandon into the house, instead of keeping him above the garage like storage. What must he think of you? And of me? He's your son, and I treated him like a common handyman!"

"He doesn't know he's my son."

Jen took a long, slow sip of her champagne and thought about what this meant. She cleared her throat and asked, "Tell me, luv. Are you still in love with Sharon?"

"Whatever Sharon and I had was over more than twenty-five years ago, so forget it."

"I can, but can you?"

"Jen, I already have."

She smiled. "I hope so. Now, try your champagne."

"It's grape juice."

"Can't you pretend? This should be a celebration."

The telephone rang in the kitchen, but neither of them paid it any attention.

"Celebrating what?" he asked, making a face as he tasted his grape juice.

"We're together. Lieutenant Hicks says you're no longer a suspect, and you have a son. That's quite a lot, don't you think?"

Margarita came in from the kitchen with a cordless phone. "Telephone, Mr. Duffy. It's Mr. Baldwin. He says it's very urgent."

Duffy took the phone from her. "Baldwin? We're in the middle of dinner."

Baldwin sounded terrible. "I was going to call you later. But I don't know what to do. It's real bad—"

"What are you talking about?"

"I'm at the Seaman place. I wanted to talk to Sharon and Brandon, but they've been drinking. They're both drunk ... dead drunk."

"Oh, shit! I'll be right over!"

———

Duffy turned into Geoff Seaman's driveway and screeched to a stop behind Baldwin's Lexus. He put the truck in park and leaped out, so fearful of what he might find that he didn't turn off the lights or the ignition. He bounded up to the front door, which was thankfully unlocked, rushed in, and ran down the hall shouting, "Baldwin! Where the hell are they?"

"In the master bedroom," Baldwin shouted back.

Duffy found him standing next to the bed where Sharon lay, stretched out on the bed, a disheveled mess. He put a hand to her throat, feeling for a pulse. It was slow—very slow and very weak.

Baldwin showed him the prescription bottle of temazepam. "I found this next to the bed. It's empty."

"Sleeping pills? Jesus! I told Brandon to clean this place out. Call 911!"

"Already did. Brandon's in the kitchen," Baldwin said, throwing his hands over his mouth. "I think he's dead."

"Oh, shit!" Duffy ran to the kitchen to find Brandon sprawled on the floor in a pool of blood. Duffy sank to his knees beside him. "Brandon! Stay with me, Brandon!"

Baldwin came up behind him. "Is he dead?"

"He's been shot in the chest!"

"Through the heart?"

Duffy felt Brandon's wrist. "God, I hope not! Who shot him?"

Baldwin pulled the .38 from his belt where his sweater had hidden it and pressed the silencer to the base of Duffy's skull. "You did."

Feeling the cold steel of the silencer, Duffy froze. "Me?"

"That's what the man said! Now, get up. Slowly. I want you to sit in one of the chairs."

Duffy didn't comprehend at first. "Look. I didn't do it. How could I? You're my lawyer! I was at dinner! Oh, God, he's my son! Please help him—"

There was a click as Baldwin cocked the .38's hammer. "Get up! And keep your cool. This is your gun—you know it has a hair trigger."

Duffy rose to his feet, slowly, deliberately, both hands high above his head. "Mine? How did you get it?"

"God, your wife's right. You are stupid." Baldwin jabbed him in the ribs with the .38, prodding him to a sunspace chair. "Sit. Hey, there's some vodka left if you want it."

"What? Jen?" Duffy was distracted by the gun in his back. "Okay, okay. Take it easy." Duffy sank down on the chair, his back to Baldwin, staring at the growing pool of Brandon's blood at his feet. "When did you call 911?"

"I didn't."

"But they'll both die—why them?"

"Consider it God's will. Part of his master plan."

"Jesus Christ! You're out of your fucking mind!"

"Brilliant." Baldwin pressed the tip of the silencer against Duffy's temple.

"Wait!"

"Sorry. You've wasted enough of my time."

Baldwin pulled the trigger. There was a deafening click as the reload misfired. Duffy's right hand shot out, grabbing Baldwin by the balls. The lawyer screamed, a look of anguish on his face as he swung his arm up to smash Duffy in the face with the butt of the gun. Duffy leaped to his feet, his right hand squeezing harder and harder. He shouldered Baldwin against the wall, yanked up on his scrotum, hoisting him to the tips of his toes. Another scream, and the .38 clattered to the floor. Duffy smashed his left fist against Baldwin's nose. Again and again, his fist smashed the lawyer's face, pounding him to the floor at Brandon's feet.

———

Duffy's Navigator was still parked behind Baldwin's Lexus, blocking the driveway, when Hicks pulled up to the curb in front of Geoff Seaman's house.

"Looks like Sharon's having a party," Torres said as he climbed out the driver's door.

"That Duffy's SUV?" Fahey asked.

"Looks like it," Hicks said.

"Must've been in a hurry," Torres said. "Engine's still running."

Fahey looked at the house. "Front door's open."

"Oh shit." Hicks said, running up the walk and through the open door. They heard a sharp thumping sound and a terrified voice yelling, "No! No! For God's sake, stop!"

"Some party!" Fahey said, pulling the Beretta out of the holster at the back of her belt. They rushed down the hall toward the sound. Duffy was on top of Baldwin in the kitchen, banging his head into the floor.

Fahey dropped to a crouch, holding her gun in both hands. "Freeze!"

Baldwin gasped, "Get him off me! Get him off!"

Torres and Hicks grabbed Duffy under his arms and pulled him up and away from Baldwin. Duffy didn't resist.

"Thank God!" Duffy panted as Hicks and Torres slammed him against the wall. Fahey holstered her gun and pulled out her cuffs.

"Don't let him go!" Baldwin shouted, struggling to his feet, clutching his throat. "He's crazy! He tried to kill me!"

"He's the crazy one!" Duffy grunted.

Torres kneed him in the kidneys. "Shut up!"

Hicks held Duffy's arms behind his back while Fahey snapped on the cuffs. Baldwin staggered around the kitchen's center island to where Duffy's .38 had fallen. Brandon let out a low groan. Fahey turned to the sound, and for the first time saw Cash's body lying in a pool of blood. She rushed passed Baldwin to Cash.

"Hey, this guy's been shot," she shouted, kneeling beside him.

"Ooh! Someone call 911," Baldwin sang, picking up the .38.

"Watch him!" Duffy warned.

Baldwin grabbed Fahey by the hair and yanked her to her feet, pressing the silencer to her head. He spun her around until they faced Hicks and Torres. "Okay! This is much better," he shouted. "Now, back off or I'll blow the bitch's fucking brains out!"

"Hold still, Red," Torres said, raising his hands.

Hicks released his grip on Duffy's arm and raised his hands. "We're cool. Just tell us what you want us to do."

"Put your weapons on the island," Baldwin ordered.

"You're an attorney, Mr. Baldwin," Hicks said. "You know we can't surrender our weapons."

"I'll kill her ..." Baldwin yanked her hair again, snapping her head back.

"Boss?" she gasped.

Torres took his Glock M17 from his shoulder holster and placed it on the island. Hicks stood his ground, giving Baldwin an icy stare.

"Do it, Lieutenant. Do it *now*, or she's dead pork." Baldwin snarled.

"If you do, the crazy bastard will kill us all," Duffy warned.

Hicks hesitated for a moment. There was a cold click as Baldwin cocked the hammer of the .38. Hicks removed his service revolver from his shoulder holster and placed it on the island next to Torres' Glock.

"Good piggies!" Baldwin barked. "Everybody, face the wall and put your hands behind your heads."

One by one, he patted the detectives down, feeling for other weapons. He was especially thorough with Fahey.

"Get a good feel. I'm the last woman you'll ever touch," she said, trying to keep her left side away from him.

He found the small spraycan of pepper spray at the front of Fahey's belt. "Ugly bitch," he snarled in her ear. He tossed the can into the sunspace, then he grabbed Torres's Glock. "Into the living room. All of you."

———

Baldwin lined them up in front of the fireplace.

"You can't kill us all," Hicks warned.

"One of us will get you," Torres said.

"Shut up," Baldwin snapped.

Hicks tried to reason with him. "Let's talk before you do something stupid."

Baldwin's eyes were darting about the room. "You're the ones who are stupid. You know what I'm going to do? I'm going to stage a good, old-fashioned gun battle. First I'll kill the three of you with Duffy's gun. Then I'll kill him with one of yours. How do you like that for a game plan?"

"Game plans don't always work," Hicks answered.

"Well, just for the fun of it, I think I'll kill the girl first."

"Asshole!" Torres shouted.

Baldwin glared at him. "Or, maybe the runt of the litter should go first?"

Torres shrugged and grinned. "Suits me fine."

He waved the Glock at Torres. "A volunteer? How noble." Baldwin glanced at Fahey, saying, "If he wasn't about to die, I'd say that you owe him a good fuck." To Torres, he ordered, "Stand in front of the couch."

Torres did as he was told, slowly moving to the couch. "This okay?"

"Perfect." Baldwin pulled the trigger. The bullet slammed into Torres's chest and a burst of air erupted from his lungs. He was slammed backward onto the couch.

Fahey screamed.

Duffy gasped.

Hicks yelled, "Jesus Christ!"

"Him? Oh, no! The Lord can't save you now," Baldwin ranted. He turned his back on Torres and nodded toward one of the Chippendale chairs flanking a game table.

"Now, Lieutenant Hicks, I'd like you over there."

Behind him, Torres's eyes fluttered open and his hand inched down his leg and slipped the switchblade knife from his boot top.

There was a click as the blade snapped open.

As Baldwin started to turn toward the sound, Torres jammed the knife to the hilt into his right buttock.

"Ow, fuck! What the—" Baldwin screamed, dropping Duffy's

.38 and grasping for the knife in his hip.

"Gotcha, asshole!" Torres grunted.

Hicks kicked the Glock out of Baldwin's other hand. Duffy dove for his .38 while Hicks scrambled for his own. Baldwin yanked the bloody switchblade from his ass and grabbed a fist full of Fahey's hair, pressing the bloody switchblade to her throat. "Stand back!" he shouted, limping, and dragging her toward the hall.

"It's over," Hicks warned, aiming his .38.

Baldwin shouted, "I'll slit her throat from ear to ear."

Hicks gripped the .38 with both hands and cocked it. "Let her go."

"Drop it, or she's bacon!"

"Don't do it boss!" Fahey cried. "Shoot this fucker!"

Baldwin began to draw the knife across her neck, starting a dark line of blood. Hicks cursed and dropped his weapon to the floor.

"Stay back! Don't try to follow us!" Baldwin ordered. He pulled Fahey out the front door and down the drive, the knife still pressed to her throat.

Duffy's Navigator was still behind his Lexus, engine running, blocking the drive. He pushed Fahey through the driver's side door, shoving her across the center console. Scrambling in after her, he jammed the shift into reverse. She tried opening her door to jump out; but he stabbed the knife blade through her left hand, pinning it to the padded dash.

"Motherfucker!" she yelled.

"Watch your fucking mouth! And fasten your seatbelt," Baldwin sneered. He backed out of the driveway and rear-ended Hicks' Yukon, ramming it three times until its left rear tire blew with a sound like a gunshot, then he shifted into drive and floored it. With a screech of burning rubber, the Navigator roared toward Sunset Boulevard.

27

Ben Jackson was driving east on Sunset, following his GPS to Geoffrey Seaman's place. Jerry Perz was sitting beside him, trying to find the same address in Jackson's street map atlas.

"I think the best way to get to Bellagio is to turn right at the next light," Perz said as they rounded a curve and headed downhill. When they reached Beverly Glen, they had the green light. As Jackson turned onto the street, a black Lincoln Navigator roared by them in the southbound lane.

"Crazy son-of-bitch," Jackson swore, swerving with a hard right to avoid getting hit.

Perz got a good look at the driver by the light of sodium vapor streetlights. "Hey!" he yelled, "That's him! That's him!"

"Who?"

"The asshole that murdered my brother!"

Jackson spun the Ford around in a skidding 180-degree pursuit turn. The Navigator ran the red light, turning west on Sunset. "Perz! You sure?"

"Sure as shit! It's the same SUV! It's him!"

Jackson floored the accelerator and swerved right onto Sunset, almost sideswiping a Rolls Royce. The speedometer climbed to eighty as they wove through the traffic after the Navigator. Jackson was too busy to pick up the mike and call for help.

"Shouldn't you turn on the siren?" Perz pleaded.

"No way! I'm way out of my territory!"

They sped around the curves of Sunset's steep hills, passing the UCLA campus on the left and the Bel Air Country Club on the right. Jackson's souped-up Ford caught up to the Navigator as they passed the Sunset entrance to UCLA.

"Hey, there's a woman with him," Perz said.

The Navigator swerved left into oncoming traffic to pass a limousine, and Jackson swerved right, passing the limo and pulling abreast of the SUV in the left lane.

"Oh, shit!" Jackson said, easing up on the accelerator. "He has Red!"

Jackson dropped a car length behind the Navigator, following it up a curving hill, doing ninety.

"We're going to kill somebody!" Perz shouted, tightening his seatbelt.

The Navigator's brake lights went on.

"Son of a bitch!" Jackson jammed down the brake pedal. They rear-ended the Navigator, bouncing off its bumper. Jackson fought for control. "Bastard's going to puncture our radiator!"

The Navigator veered left, through three lanes of oncoming traffic, roaring south on Veteran.

"This is crazy!" Perz shouted, nearly crying as Jackson pursued the SUV by pushing it up to eighty again. "It's not worth it! Let him go!"

"Perz!" Jackson shouted back. "That's my detective up there. And no asshole in an SUV gonna outrun me!"

They raced down Veteran almost bumper-to-bumper. The street jogged left at the Los Angeles National Cemetery. A pickup pulled into the left lane cutting off the Navigator. The SUV swerved right and suddenly went out of control, flipping into the cemetery, tearing up the grass and shattering the neat symmetry of the rows of military grave markers in a cloud of flying sod and chips of white marble. A body flew out the sunroof. The SUV rolled over it and tumbled on for almost another fifty yards before coming to a stop, upside-down on its flattened roof.

Jackson ran over the curb and swerved into the cemetery, braking to a stop. He jumped out, tossing his cell phone to Perz, yelling, "Call 911! Tell 'em to get the medics here fast! A police officer's down!"

Jackson ran along the trail of rubble where the SUV had ripped through the graves, not bothering to stop when he sprinted past the crushed body that had been expelled through the sunroof. It was a male, and he knew without checking that the man was beyond help.

Smoke and steam were rising from the SUV's crushed engine compartment when Jackson arrived. He could smell the gasoline from the ruptured fuel tank that was leaking into the front seat.

"Red!" Jackson shouted, dropping to his knees beside what was left of the passenger side door.

"What's up, Ben," Fahey whispered.

The roof of the Navigator had been crushed to within eighteen inches of the floor. Jackson turned on his flashlight and shined it inside. Fahey's upside down face smiled back at him, the straps of her seat belt and the crushed roof holding her in the fetal position.

"You okay?" he asked.

"It's a little cramped in here." She sniffed and her voice quivered. "Jesus, Ben! Is that gas?"

"Are you ... uh, can you move?"

"Yeah. I can wiggle my fingers and toes."

"Okay. Screw the medics, I'm getting you out of there." He reached inside and tried to unfasten her seat belt, but couldn't reach it.

Fahey managed to inch her hand to the buckle, and told Ben, "I'll fall, okay? Hold me!"

He put his big hands under her head and shoulders. She released the seat belt and dropped into his arms. With all his strength, he tried pulling her through the opening of the shattered window. The smell of gasoline was getting stronger.

"Ow! Goddamn it! My fucking foot's caught!"

Jackson had her halfway out. Hooking his arms under hers, he clasped his hands across her chest.

"Easy with the girls, Ben," she joked, laughing and limp in his arms. He merely grunted, placed his feet against the SUV's side for leverage, and pulled.

"Hey! You're tearing off my fucking shoe!"

"Good!" He yanked her free and they both tumbled backward.

"My shoe! I lost ..." Jackson picked her up, and she passed out in his arms. He began to run. The Navigator exploded in an orange ball of flame.

28

If Matthew Baldwin had lived, he would have discovered how wrong he'd been earlier that evening. It didn't turn out to be a beautiful night in Los Angeles. Long jagged fingers of lightning streaked the sky as El Niño prepared to attack the city again. The rain began to fall a few minutes after Baldwin's crushed remains were zipped into a body bag and hoisted like a sack of potatoes into the back of a Medical Examiner's van for the ride to the L.A. County Morgue.

In Bel Air, the rain soaked the small army of men and women marching in and out of Geoffrey Seaman's house from the emergency vehicles that lined the driveway and street.

When the first paramedics arrived on the scene, Sharon and Cash were comatose. Brandon was bagged and CPR was started. A medic cut away his sweatshirt, located the entrance and exit wounds, and normalized his breathing. A large IV tube bored into his right arm. Sharon was given pure oxygen and amps of Narcan and D50. Both arms were pierced with IVs and saline drips were started. Once stabilized, mother and son were strapped to gurneys, and a frenzy of paramedics hurried them across the lawn in the downpour, shielding them with umbrellas and holding their IV bags and oxygen bottles. The gurneys were pushed into a waiting white and red medic van, and the instant the rear doors slammed shut, the van roared off to the Cedars-Sinai Medical Center, sirens wailing and emergency lights flashing.

As the sirens faded away, Gordon Duffy was still being interviewed by a team of LAPD detectives. Hicks stood in the living room, watching an attractive female medic check out Torres as he lay on the couch, naked from the waist up, while she probed his ribs with her fingers.

"Jesus, go easy." Torres complained. "I'm not into the rough stuff. This hurts like hell!"

The medic smiled and took a roll of two-inch tape from her medical kit. "It'll be that way for a few of days. You probably have a couple of cracked ribs."

"Hey, hear that?" he asked Hicks. "I could use a little time off."

"It might be arranged." Hicks gave his shoulder a pat. "That took a lot of guts, Torres."

"Stupidity," Torres disagreed. "I thought the reloads in Duffy's gun would misfire. They didn't."

Hicks smiled. "He used your Glock, Luis."

"Lucky you were wearing that Kevlar," the medic said.

"Not luck. I wouldn't be seen dead without it."

"He likes the way it makes him look," Hicks said to the medic. She gently patted Torres' chest. "Oh, like a Wonder Bra?"

"Saved my life!" Torres said.

"We'll have to take you in for some x-rays," the medic said, packing up her kit. "You could have some fractured ribs, maybe even a hematoma in the clavicle region."

"Interesting. What does that mean in English?" Torres asked.

"You could die, smartass."

———

A beefy LAPD detective stalked into the living room from the kitchen, cell phone in hand. "Okay, who's Hicks?" his voice boomed.

"Here," Hicks said.

"Mike Quinn," the detective said with a toothy grin. He extended a meaty paw to Hicks. "Little out of your territory, ain't ya'?"

"A little," Hicks admitted.

"I just arrived on the scene," Quinn hitched up his pants, exposing the LAPD Captain's shield on his belt. "My guys say ya' told them the perp got away in a blue Lincoln SUV?"

"Black," Hicks aid. "And he took one of my deputies as a hostage."

"Well, the asshole didn't get far."

"You got him?"

"No, one of your men did. Sergeant Jackson? He pursued the perp down Sunset at speeds up to ninety." He shook his head and his double chin jiggled. "Shit, man. Don't you people in the sticks know there's a statute against high-speed police pursuits in congested urban areas? Kill a citizen chasing a perp and you could face a homicide charge yourself. Your fucking sergeant should've let the asshole go. Jackson's one lucky son-of-a-bitch, I tell you. That asshole could've killed more people than he did—"

"Jackson killed someone?"

"Not Jackson; the fucking perp. He lost control doing about eighty on Veteran. It rolled five or six times and ended up in L.A. National Cemetery. Good place for it, if you ask me. Fucking SUVs aren't worth a shit on the road. Damn thing took out a couple dozen grave markers before it blew up like a napalm bomb. One occupant was thrown from the vehicle; head was crushed like an egg. Died instantly. Other guy should've bought the farm, too."

"Guy?"

"Yeah, your deputy? Fahey? Anyway, that's the name they gave me on the phone."

A wave of relief swept over Hicks. "Fahey's a woman."

Quinn scratched his ass. "A broad? No kidding."

"She all right?"

"As far as I know, she only has a stab wound in the hand. The perp's knife went right through it without hitting a bone or a tendon. Luck of the Irish, I guess."

"I guess," Hicks said.

"The medics strapped her to a body board—just as a precaution, you know—and took her to UCLA for observation. Jackson's with her. Give him a call; he can fill you in." Quinn took out a leather case and handed Hicks his card. "That's my number if you need anything. Now, if it's okay with you, I'd like to get my guys out of here. Half of 'em are on overtime, and I can already feel HR crawling up my ass about it."

"You're not claiming jurisdiction?" Hicks asked with surprise, walking the detective captain to the door.

"Hell, no!" Quinn grinned. "You're welcome to the fucking paperwork." He winked at Hicks. "Of course, I could change my mind if Sharon Grant or the kid with the hole in his chest go and kick off."

"Let's hope they don't," Hicks said.

"You're telling me! The media would shit themselves. I'm not releasing any names to the fuckers tonight; let the day guys handle those celebrity-crazed assholes. Okay with you?"

Hicks nodded. "I'd like to get home tonight."

Quinn clapped Hicks on the back. "Well, let me know if I can be of any more help. Hear?"

"There's one thing I could use," Hicks said.

"Name it, you got it."

"Service truck. The perp rammed into my truck and blew out my rear tire. I have to get it fixed."

"Done," Quinn said

"Thanks," Hicks said.

"Forget it," Quinn said, pulling up the collar of his black and white houndstooth jacket. "You owe me one."

———

The paramedics took Torres to the UCLA Center for x-rays. It was almost an hour before Hicks could call Ben Jackson to find out that

Fahey seemed okay, but they wanted to keep her under observation for a couple more hours.

"What about Torres?" Hicks asked.

"Well, they're being careful with him. Sometimes it doesn't pay to be a cop. The docs got into a big argument about what to do with him. The long and the short of it is they decided x-rays or even a CT couldn't always detect a possible great vessel injury, so they're giving him the works—x-rays, CT, plus something called an aortogram— just to be safe. If everything's okay, we could be out of there by midnight."

"Is Perz still with you?"

"Naw. I drove him to the airport while they were checking Red. He's a little shook, but a real gutsy guy. We ought to see if our canine guys have a German shepherd pup we can give him."

Just after 10:30 p.m., the LAPD service truck had Hicks's Yukon ready to roll and the crime scene was secured. Hicks left two uniformed officers from the West L.A. police division guarding the Seaman residence and drove Duffy home. Both men were dead tired, and not a word was exchanged between them during the four-block drive. The rain had stopped by the time they turned into Duffy's driveway, but occasional flashes of lightning still streaked the eastern sky.

"It's been a long day," Duffy finally said as Hicks stopped halfway up the drive. He paused, then asked, "What are you going to do about Jen?"

Hicks smiled. "Tonight, she's your problem."

Duffy was surprised. "But I thought you'd take her in for questioning."

"Look. I've got two deputies in the hospital. If they're okay, I'm going home and getting some sleep. Tomorrow, I'll talk to the D.A. If he thinks we have a case against her, I'll be back to pick her up."

Duffy nodded. "I kind of wish you'd take her now."

"All we can do is wait. Sorry it's going to be a rough night for you."

"I know. I still love her."

———

Hicks pulled up to the UCLA Medical Center emergency entrance, checked in with reception, and found Fahey's room. She was lying on a gurney, still strapped to a backboard. Ben Jackson was at her side.

"How's it going?" Hicks asked.

She rolled her eyes. "Terrific, boss! My fucking back feels like a dream."

He took her hand. "I thought they said you weren't hurt that bad."

Jackson grinned. "She's not. They're almost ready to discharge her."

"Yeah?" Fahey said. "That's easy for you to say. You've never been strapped to one of these goddamn boards. It's worse than the rack." She held up her bandaged hand. "And look at my poor hand. That asshole Baldwin really nailed me."

A nurse bustled into the room. "The doctors told me to get rid of you. You can go home," she told Fahey cheerily. She nodded at Hicks and Jackson, pulling a curtain around the bed. "Now, if you gentlemen will step into the hall, I'll unstrap your lady friend."

"Be careful," Hicks warned, "she's no lady."

"Yeah," Jackson said. "She's a trained killer."

While they were standing outside Fahey's room, two automatic doors at the end of the hall banged opened and a nurse pushed a wheelchair toward them. "Hey!" Torres yelled from the chair, "All my tests were negative! I'm gonna live!"

They checked out of the hospital at midnight and drove back to San Bernardino.

29

The next afternoon, Hicks had a 3:00 appointment with Assistant District Attorney Joe Walker. It turned out to be such a beautiful day, he decided to walk the mile from his office to the District Attorney's offices. Although it was the middle of January, the air was soft and sweet, with a hint of spring. The view was one-of-a-kind; at least, it was that afternoon. El Niño had swept the smog out of the valley, and the snow-covered peaks of the mountains to the north of the city stood out brilliantly against the cobalt sky.

Shortly after three, Hicks was briefing the young assistant district attorney, who sat impassively behind his massive desk, the tips of his fingers pressed together, listening intently.

"So that's it," Hicks finally finished. "You probably think I'm a royal screw-up for letting Baldwin almost kill us all."

"Why would I think that? You got Baldwin."

"By accident. Christ, I was so sure it was Brandon Cash. If we hadn't gone to pick him up—"

"Doesn't matter. You got the son-of-a-bitch. I always thought Matt was a freak. He kept himself pretty much under control with medication in law school, but once in a while, he'd purposely go off it. Said he missed the highs. I sure as hell never dreamed he was capable of murdering three people."

"Four," Hicks corrected him.

"Did Grant or the kid die?"

Hicks shook his head. "Baldwin murdered his own mother with the .38 he switched with Duffy's. He blew her away on the streets of San Francisco to make it appear to be a random drive-by shooting. And there may be others. We're checking with all the Los Angles and Bay Area law enforcement agencies."

"I don't get it. Why would Baldwin switch the guns? I mean, the crazy son-of-a-bitch must have known you'd run ballistic tests on it."

"Lots of things Baldwin did don't make sense. The LAPD found a rental receipt for the Navigator he used the night of the murders. He rented it at the Ontario Airport with his own credit card and picked it up around 6:00 that evening. I guess he had ordered a black one and got pissed when the only color available was dark blue. Then, he had another argument when he returned it at 2:00 in the morning, claiming that the scratches on the back fender were there when he picked it up. Maybe he wanted to get caught. Or maybe he was just playing games with us."

"How are Fahey and Torres doing?"

"They're okay. I gave them a couple of days off."

"And Grant and the kid? They going to make it?"

Hicks nodded. "I checked with Cedars-Sinai just before I left my office. Sharon's off the critical list. She's lucky she was an alcoholic."

"Lucky?"

"Her high tolerance probably saved her. And Baldwin made another big mistake: temazepam is a generic form of Restoril. They're not barbiturates; you could down a hundred capsules and still survive. Mixing them with alcohol isn't good, but the medics were able to pump her stomach and neutralize them before they did too much damage. Basically, once Grant was intubated and stabilized all she needed to do was sleep it off. Still, I bet she had one bitch of a hangover this morning."

"And Brandon?"

"Still critical, but he's young and will probably survive. The slug went right through him, missing most of the major vessels and lungs. When the surgeons cracked him open, they found a tear in an artery above the armpit, but they rebuilt it with a section of vein from his leg. Nurse said he's alert and talking. Looks like you won't have another murder to prosecute."

"Everyone was very lucky last night."

"Everyone but Baldwin. And hopefully Jennifer Duffy."

"I'll have to discuss it with the D.A., but personally, I'm not sure we can or will do anything about her."

"Jesus, Joe! You saying you won't indict her?"

"I'd love to. I'd love to put her in the hole for life, but I'm not sure it's worth the effort."

"That's as insane as Baldwin!"

"Look, Len. From all you've told me, we really don't have much of a case against her."

"Bullshit. She's guilty as Baldwin. They planned everything together. We both know it. All you have to do is convince a jury."

"Yeah, but I doubt we could prove that she helped Baldwin plan anything."

"She sure as hell was a co-conspirator. She sure as hell was fucking around with Baldwin. She had to know that he was crazy. Shit, she probably used him to kill Shelton and nail her husband for it. Eventually, she'd get everything he had. But the game went to hell—she didn't know Duffy had a son, and Baldwin didn't play by the rules. To him, murder was the name of the game. So don't kid yourself, Joe. She's guilty as him. I'd bet my career on it."

"And you'd probably win," Walker agreed. "But if the only witness against her is her husband who loves her, I'd bet my ass she'll make sure he doesn't change his mind. He can't be forced to testify against his wife."

"Maybe he'll come to his senses."

"Doesn't matter. Duffy could divorce her, and she'll still have her GameCo stock and plenty of money to buy her way out of any trial. Her lawyers will put Duffy on the stand as a hostile witness and tear him apart."

"But she can't explain the gun switch." Hicks said.

"She'll just say Baldwin asked her to make the switch to protect her husband. Look, I'll let you know what the D.A. decides, but the bottom line is that it could cost the state a small fortune to try her ... but she'll probably walk."

Hicks got up to leave.

Walker stopped him with one last question. "If Deputy Fahey were a guy, would you have surrendered your weapon and let Baldwin leave that house?"

With a small shrug, Hicks shook his head and said, "Probably not."

Fuck literature.

www.contemporarypress.com

Current Titles

Dead Dog by Mike Segretto: A curmudgeonly shut-in's life is turned inside-out when he becomes involved with a trash-talking femme fatale, a trio of psychotic gangsters, and a dog whose incessant barking has caused him years of sleepless nights. Spiked with ample doses of sex, violence and campy humor, *Dead Dog* is a riotous road trip from an Arizona trailer park to hell.
ISBN 0-9744614-0-7

Down Girl by Jess Dukes: In *Down Girl*, 29-year-old Pauline Rose Lennon works too hard for every cent she ever made until she meets Anton, willing to give her more cash than she's ever imagined...for one small favor. Pauline's life spins hilariously out of control, but she pulls it back from the brink just in time to prove that just because you're down, it doesn't mean you're out.
ISBN 0-9744614-1-5

Johnny Astronaut by Rory Carmichael: In the future, disco is king. *Johnny Astronaut* is the story of a hard-boiled, hard-drinking P.I. who stumbles upon a mysterious book that changes his life forever. Caught between a vindictive ex-wife, a powerful crime boss, and a sinister race of lizard people, Johnny becomes embroiled in a fast-paced, hilarious adventure that stretches across space and time.
ISBN 0-9744614-3-1

G.O.P. D.O.A. by Jay Brida: While the city braces for 20,000 Republicans to descend on New York, a Brooklyn political operative named Flanagan uncovers a bizarre plot that could trigger a Red, White, Black and Blue nightmare. Populated by buffoons, hacks, thugs and the Sons of Joey Ramone, *G.O.P. D.O.A.* is a fast paced, ripping yarn that gorges on the American buffet of sexual hypocrisy, political ambition and the Republican way of life.
ISBN 0-9744614-5-8

How To Smash Everyone To Pieces by Mike Segretto: Ex-stunt woman, mass murderer, and champion wise-cracker Mary is furious to discover that her twin sister Desiree—accused of murdering her husband—has been wrangled back to an Arizona prison by a grizzled detective named Tuttle. Fueled by an unnaturally obsessive love for her twin, Mary sets off on a homicidal cross-country campaign to free Desiree from the clutches of the law, recruiting a bizarre bunch of cohorts on the way.

Exploding with action, uproarious one-liners, and more cartoon violence than an episode of Tom and Jerry, *How to Smash Everyone to Pieces* is one of the most perverse and hilarious tales ever to come tearing down the highway.
ISBN 0-9744614-6-6

Contemporary Press (est. 2003) is committed to truth, justice and going our own way. When Big Publishing dies, we're the cockroaches who will devour their bones and dance on their graves.